# The Perfect Sting

**A TORLAN TARSEN ADVENTURE**

# The Perfect Sting

Russell V McFall

*Ordained Path Books*

Published by **Ordained Path Books**
For permissions or inquiries, contact:
**ordainedpathbooks@gmail.com**

Cover illustration and interior artwork generated by AI under direction of the author.

**First Edition**

**ISBN (Paperback):** 978-1-972724-20-0
**ISBN (Hardcover)**:

Printed in the United States of America.

Version 1.00 - -May 2026

# Dedication

*For those who know*
*the right way is not always the easiest—*
*but it is always worth finding.*

# Contents

## Chapter 1 - Return to the Estate

Torlan's estate always seemed quieter after trouble.

Not peaceful exactly. Peace was too soft a word for a place like this. The grounds were too carefully kept, the drives too clean, the wide lawns too evenly trimmed beneath the evening lights. Even the old stone walls seemed disciplined, as though instructed long ago never to lean, crumble, or complain.

But it was quiet.

That was enough for tonight.

A low wind moved across the dark grass beyond the windows of the main study. Inside, a fire burned with a steady glow, throwing warm light across shelves of old books, polished wood, and a long table now covered with documents, data slates, printouts, and one very stubborn tea tray that had been pushed aside three times and kept drifting back toward the center as if it wanted to be part of the investigation.

Marcus stood near the fireplace with his arms folded.

Alexa sat at the far end of the table, one knee tucked beneath her chair, eyes narrowed at the screen in front of her. She had been quiet for nearly ten minutes, which usually meant she was either thinking hard or preparing to say something no one wanted to hear.

Torlan stood at the head of the table.

He had not sat down since the meeting began.

That told everyone more than his words had.

The Halvern matter was supposed to be finished. The arrests had been made. The false trails had been traced. The immediate danger had passed —or at least that was what the final report claimed in its careful, official language.

Immediate danger passed.

Torlan had never liked that phrase.

It always sounded like someone describing a fire while standing in smoke.

Marcus tapped one finger against his sleeve. "You have read this section three times."

Torlan looked up. "Four."

"That is not comforting."

"No," Torlan said. "It is not."

Alexa turned her screen slightly so the others could see. "The name appears in three places. Not as a signer. Not as an owner. Not as a listed partner. It is buried in routing notes and transfer approvals."

"Kessler," Marcus said.

Alexa nodded. "Rovan Kessler."

The name sat in the room like a stone dropped into still water.

No one spoke for a moment.

Torlan turned one of the printed sheets toward himself. "He was careful."

"Careful men make boring criminals," Marcus said. "I miss boring criminals."

Alexa gave him a sideways look. "You have never missed a criminal in your life."

"I miss the concept."

Torlan almost smiled, but not quite.

That was another sign.

Marcus noticed.

"So," Marcus said more quietly, "what is he?"

Torlan looked back at the scattered records.

"That," he said, "is the problem."

He picked up one sheet. "Halvern used shell transfers, false contract assignments, and reclassification filings. We followed those. We thought we had reached the top of the structure."

"But we did not," Alexa said.

"No." Torlan lowered the page. "We touched the edge of a machine."

The room grew still again.

Outside, the wind moved softly against the glass.

Marcus unfolded his arms. "A machine."

"A larger structure," Torlan said. "Organized. Protected. Designed so that the people using it may not even understand the whole of it."

Alexa leaned forward. "Halvern was not the architect. He was a user."

"And Kessler?" Marcus asked.

Torlan looked at the name again.

"Kessler may be the man who built the system."

Marcus let out a slow breath. "That is not a small accusation."

"No," Torlan said. "Which is why it cannot be treated like one."

Alexa tapped her screen and brought up a financial map. Lines spread across the display like thin veins of light. Companies. Holdings. Transfers. Disputed contracts. Trade registrations.

At the center of several quiet connections stood one name.

Kessler.

Not bold.

Not obvious.

That somehow made it worse.

"He does not appear where powerful men usually appear," Alexa said. "No speeches. No bright public claims. No grand announcements."

"Then where is he?" Marcus asked.

"In the corrections," she said. "The adjustments. The final approvals no one reads unless something goes wrong."

Torlan nodded. "That is where intelligent control hides."

Marcus looked from Alexa to Torlan. "You both sound as though you admire him."

"I understand him," Torlan said.

"That is worse."

This time Torlan did smile faintly. "Possibly."

Alexa closed one file and opened another. "Profitthorn is the common point."

"The trade hub?" Marcus asked.

"Yes. Exchange Spire in particular. Kessler operates from there, though not always directly. His companies orbit it. His people move through it. His money touches it."

Marcus came closer to the table. "Then we send the report to the authorities there."

Alexa shook her head before Torlan could answer.

Marcus noticed. "That was too hopeful, was it?"

"Yes," Alexa said.

Torlan rested both hands on the table. "If Kessler built a machine large enough to protect Halvern, then a report will not be enough. It may warn him. It may bury evidence. It may place innocent people in danger before we understand how the system works."

Marcus frowned. "So what do you suggest?"

Torlan did not answer immediately.

That was when the room changed.

Not visibly. The fire still burned. The estate still stood quiet around them. The tea still sat neglected near the center of the table.

But something had shifted.

Until that moment, they had been reviewing the past.

Now Torlan was deciding the future.

"We go to Profitthorn," he said.

Marcus looked at him sharply. "We?"

Torlan glanced at Alexa.

She already understood.

"No," Marcus said. "I know that look. That is a two-person look."

Alexa lifted one eyebrow. "There is such a thing?"

"There is when Torlan is about to be unreasonable."

Torlan straightened. "A large team would attract attention."

"A small team can disappear," Marcus said.

"A small team can observe."

"A small team can also get trapped."

Torlan accepted that with a slight nod. "Which is why we will not confront anyone. We will verify. We will learn whether Kessler is what these records suggest. If he is not, we return."

Marcus stared at him.

Alexa stared at Torlan.

Torlan looked at neither of them for a moment.

Then he added, "If he is, we find the right way to bring him down."

Marcus walked slowly around the table. "You already believe he is."

"I believe the pattern deserves investigation."

"That was a very expensive way to say yes."

Alexa almost smiled.

Torlan did not.

Marcus stopped beside the financial map. "Why Alexa?"

"Because she sees patterns most people miss," Torlan said.

Alexa looked up. "That is either a compliment or an assignment."

"Both," Torlan said.

Marcus pointed toward the display. "And what about the rest of us?"

"You remain here unless needed."

Marcus made a sound that was not quite a laugh. "Unless needed. That is a phrase people use right before they need everyone."

"Perhaps," Torlan said.

The fire shifted in the hearth. A small log cracked and settled.

For a moment no one said anything.

Then Alexa turned her screen back toward herself. "If we go in small, we need a cover strong enough to hold casual questions."

Torlan nodded. "Commercial consulting. Trade compliance. Something dull enough that no one wants to discuss it at dinner."

Marcus said, "You have a gift for making danger sound like paperwork."

"Most danger is paperwork," Alexa said.

"That is the most depressing thing I have heard tonight."

Torlan gathered the printed sheets into a neat stack. "We will need a small office once we arrive. Something close enough to observe Exchange Spire, but ordinary enough not to matter."

Alexa was already typing. "Profitthorn has rotating trade offices available for short-term lease. Most are used by brokers, auditors, negotiators, shipment reviewers—"

"Boring criminals," Marcus muttered.

"Consultants," Alexa corrected.

"Same shoes. Different invoice."

This time Torlan's smile stayed a little longer.

Then he looked back at the name.

Kessler.

The warmth of the study seemed to retreat from the table.

Marcus saw it.

"You think he is dangerous," he said.

"Yes."

"More dangerous than Halvern?"

Torlan folded the final sheet and set it atop the stack.

"Halvern wanted advantage," he said. "Kessler appears to want control."

Marcus nodded slowly. "That is worse."

"Yes."

Alexa closed the display. "When do we leave?"

"Tomorrow," Torlan said.

Marcus looked between them, then gave a reluctant sigh. "Of course tomorrow. Sensible people would say next week."

"Sensible people do not always catch machines before they move," Torlan said.

Marcus did not answer that.

The meeting broke apart slowly after that. Not because there was nothing more to say, but because everyone understood the shape of the decision now. There would be planning. Quiet departures. Messages sent through careful channels. Reservations made under ordinary names.

But the decision had already been made.

One by one, the others left the study.

Alexa stayed last.

Torlan stood by the window, looking out over the estate grounds. The lights along the drive curved away into darkness. Beyond them, the world was still and quiet and far too large to control.

Alexa came to stand beside him.

"You know Marcus is worried," she said.

"He should be."

"That is not reassuring."

"No."

She studied his face. "Are you?"

Torlan did not answer at once.

At last he said, "Yes."

Alexa looked back toward the table. "Good."

He turned slightly. "Good?"

"If you were not worried, I would be."

The faint smile returned, but the weight in his eyes remained.

Alexa folded her arms. "We go in small."

Torlan nodded.

"We observe."

"Yes."

"We verify."

"Yes."

"And if Kessler is what you think he is?"

Torlan looked out into the darkness.

"Then we do not strike at the edge," he said. "We find the center."

Alexa was quiet for a moment.

Then she said, "Let's meet the machine."

Torlan looked once more toward the darkened grounds.

The estate was quiet.

For tonight, that was enough.

Tomorrow, the machine would begin to answer.

## Chapter 2 - The Architect

Morning came to the estate with a calm that felt almost suspicious.

Torlan had always thought mornings after major decisions carried a peculiar silence, as though the world paused briefly to see whether a person meant what he had said the night before.

He did.

By sunrise the study had become less a meeting room and more a planning center.

Data slates covered the long table in ordered stacks. Financial records from the Halvern files sat cross-referenced beside shipping manifests, shell ownership maps, and three pages of notes in Alexa's neat, unforgiving handwriting.

Marcus had once said her notes looked like something a judge might use while sentencing a city.

Torlan had not disagreed.

Alexa stood at the far wall where a projection filled nearly half the room. Layers of corporate structures glowed in shifting threads of light.

At first glance it looked like chaos.

At second glance, it looked designed.

Torlan studied it with his arms folded.

"Move back two layers," he said.

Alexa made an adjustment.

Several outer companies vanished.

A smaller structure remained.

Marcus, carrying coffee and skepticism in nearly equal amounts, paused beside them.

"That looks worse."

"It is worse," Alexa said.

Marcus handed Torlan a mug. "You slept?"

"Some."

"That was not a yes."

Torlan took the coffee. "It was not."

Marcus pointed toward the projection. "Explain again why we are chasing a man hidden inside accounting footnotes."

Alexa gave him a look.

Torlan answered.

"Because intelligent predators rarely stand in doorways."

Marcus considered that.

"I preferred ordinary criminals."

"You keep saying that," Alexa said.

"I mean it every time."

She zoomed one branch of the structure larger.

A name appeared.

Rovan Kessler.

Not centered, but threaded through the structure—embedded exactly where he should not have mattered, and somehow mattered most.

Exactly where he should not have mattered—

and somehow mattered most.

Marcus frowned.

"He hides inside corrections."

Alexa nodded.

"Approvals.
Reclassifications.
Settlement revisions.
Ownership amendments."

Marcus looked at Torlan.

"And this suggests architect?"

Torlan set his coffee down.

"It suggests someone who doesn't merely use systems.
He designs where they bend."

That quieted the room.

Alexa shifted another layer.

"This interests me," she said.

A cluster of companies lit up.

Three had disappeared years earlier.

Two had merged.

Several existed only briefly.

Yet money moved through all of them.

Marcus leaned closer.

"Ghost companies."

"Possibly," Alexa said.

Torlan shook his head.

"Not ghosts.
Bridges."

Alexa glanced at him.

He pointed.

"Temporary structures built to move something across."

Marcus looked from one to the other.

"Do you two rehearse being unsettling?"

"Only before breakfast," Alexa said.

Marcus sighed.

"I miss simpler friendships."

Torlan's attention stayed on the projection.

The pattern had a shape now.

And he disliked its shape.

Not chaotic.

Intentional.

As if someone had anticipated scrutiny.

That troubled him. Deeply.

Marcus saw it.

"What?"

Torlan was quiet.

Then:

"I do not think Kessler merely protects corruption."

Marcus waited.

Torlan said,

"I think he studies systems the way engineers study load."

Marcus blinked.

"Well."

"What?"

"That may be the most alarming thing you have said yet."

Alexa folded her arms.

"He may be your mirror."

Marcus looked at her.

"I did not need to hear that."

Torlan half smiled.

But only half.

Because he had already considered it.

And disliked how plausible it felt.

Both analytical.

Both builders.

Both drawn to structure.

One using structure to preserve truth.

The other—

perhaps to bury it.

The thought lingered.

Marcus broke the silence.

"So what is the plan?"

Torlan moved toward the table.

He placed a folder before Marcus.

Inside:

Profitthorn.

Exchange Spire.

Transit schedules.

Commercial permits.

Marcus stared.

"You were preparing this before last night ended."

Torlan did not deny it.

Alexa said dryly,
"He plans while other people blink."

Marcus looked wounded.

"I blink strategically."

Torlan ignored them.

"We go in as trade compliance consultants."

Marcus nodded slowly.

"Boring enough to survive scrutiny."

"Exactly."

Alexa added,
"It gives us reason to ask questions people normally resent."

Marcus looked impressed.

"That's almost elegant."

"Almost?"

"I refuse to encourage either of you fully."

Torlan sat at last.

Rare enough Marcus noticed.

Then Torlan said what had clearly been forming all morning.

"No team."

Marcus frowned.

"We discussed that."

"We confirm it now."

He looked at both of them.

"Only Alexa and I go."

Marcus opened his mouth.

Closed it.

Opened it again.

"That remains a terrible idea."

"Likely."

"Still doing it?"

"Yes."

Marcus rubbed his forehead.

"Wonderful."

Torlan leaned forward.

"A larger team means patterns.

Patterns get seen."

Alexa nodded.

"We go in small.

Quiet.

Invisible."

Marcus looked between them.

"And if Kessler is what you think?"

Torlan answered without hesitation.

"Then we do not confront him yet."

Marcus said, "What do we do?"

Torlan looked at the glowing web of companies.

"We learn how the machine breathes."

That line sat in the room.

Even Marcus did not joke.

At length he said,

"And if the machine notices you?"

Torlan's expression barely changed.

"Then we learn that too."

Marcus muttered something about unreasonable friends and sat down heavily.

Alexa closed the projection.

The room dimmed.

Decision had settled.

Now logistics.

Travel windows were reviewed.

Cover identities tested.

Office leasing options compared.

Profitthorn maps studied.

Hours passed.

By afternoon the mission felt less like theory and more like inevitability.

Late in the day Marcus stood near the study doors while Torlan packed away the final documents.

He watched quietly.

Then said,

"You know something troubles me?"

"Several things trouble you."

Marcus ignored that.

"You sound less like a man investigating a criminal... and more like a man studying an opponent."

Torlan paused.

A fair observation.

Perhaps too fair.

At last he said:

"If Kessler built what I think he built..."

he closed the last folder,

"...then confrontation without understanding would be foolish."

Marcus nodded once.

Then:

"Just do me a favor."

"What?"

"Do not admire him."

Alexa looked up.

Torlan did too.

Marcus added quietly,

"Men sometimes become vulnerable to what they study."

That landed.

Deeper than Marcus perhaps intended.

Torlan said nothing for a long moment.

Then:

"I do not admire him."

He paused before adding,

"I intend to understand him."

Marcus pointed.

"That was almost worse."

Even Alexa laughed.

A small one.

But welcome.

Toward evening the car was prepared.

Travel arrangements finalized.

The estate staff moved with practiced discretion, asking little.

As though strange departures belonged to ordinary life here.

Perhaps they did.

At the front steps Marcus stood with them in the cooling air.

The light had begun to fade gold.

Alexa adjusted a case at her side.

Marcus looked at both of them.

"So this is it."

"For now," Torlan said.

Marcus folded his arms.

"You know what worries me most?"

Torlan waited.

Marcus nodded toward the files.

"That you may actually find the machine."

Torlan looked toward the waiting car.

Then back.

"No," he said quietly.

"What worries me most…"

he opened the car door,

"…is that we already have."

They stood in silence.

Wind moved lightly through the trees.

Then Alexa smiled faintly.

"Well."

Marcus looked at her.

"Well what?"

She stepped toward the car.

"Let's meet the machine."

And with that—
they left for Profitthorn.

## Chapter 3 - Arrival at Profitthorn

Profitthorn appeared first as geometry.

From a distance, as the transport descended through upper traffic lanes, the trade hub seemed less a city than a calculation someone had persuaded into architecture.

Lines. Angles. Movement. Order.

Massive shipping corridors crossed one another in luminous strands. Cargo lifts climbed the sides of towered depots. Freight gliders drifted between loading spires with mechanical precision, their movements so measured they seemed choreographed.

Nothing looked accidental.

Torlan watched through the transport window without speaking.

Alexa, beside him, was studying the city with the particular expression she wore when trying to decide whether something was impressive or suspicious.

With Alexa, the two often overlapped.

After a while she said, "Either this place is remarkably efficient…"

Torlan waited.

"…or deeply controlling."

He gave the slightest nod.

"Possibly both."

She glanced at him.

"That was not comforting."

"Profit rarely seeks comfort."

She leaned back.

"You have become unusually philosophical for a man entering potential criminal territory."

Torlan looked down toward the immense hub.

"Perhaps I'm trying to sound calm."

"Is it working?"

"No."

Alexa seemed satisfied by that.

Below them, the city widened.

Trade districts unfolded in ordered bands. Markets clustered in concentric zones. Transit channels pulsed with constant motion.

At the center of it all—

rising above nearly everything—

stood Exchange Spire.

Even from the transport, it dominated the skyline.

Not the tallest structure in Profitthorn.

But unmistakably the center.

Its upper glass caught morning light in hard silver planes. Lower levels spread into adjoining commercial towers linked by enclosed bridges and transit connectors.

A city within the city.

Alexa looked at it and said softly,

"Well."

Torlan almost smiled.

"Yes."

"That must be it."

"It is."

She was quiet for several seconds.

Then:

"I dislike buildings that look as though they know something."

"That may be unfair to architecture."

"I'm willing to risk offending architecture."

The transport banked lower.

Docking approach began.

A voice announced arrivals in a tone so cheerful it made Marcus's absence suddenly feel unfortunate.

He would have mocked it immediately.

Torlan almost missed that.

Almost.

The transport settled.

Their arrival was uneventful.

Which, for present purposes, was ideal.

They stepped into a transit concourse alive with movement.

Merchants.

Auditors.

Couriers.

Negotiators.

The air carried overlapping voices, moving machinery, faint electrical hums, and the smell of too much coffee trying heroically to hold civilization together.

Alexa stopped once simply to watch people.

Torlan noticed.

"What?"

She nodded toward the crowd.

"No one strolls."

He looked.

She was right.

Everyone moved with purpose.

Not hurried.

Directed.

A subtle difference.

Torlan said,

"Trade hubs worship momentum."

Alexa frowned.

"That sounds unhealthy."

"Most religions become so."

She gave him a look.

"You are definitely being philosophical."

He took that as accusation.

They moved toward the commercial district assigned for temporary firms.

Their cover had been arranged under an intentionally unremarkable name:

**Meridian Trade Compliance Associates.**

Alexa had objected only that it sounded "like paperwork wearing shoes."

Torlan had taken that as approval.

Their leased offices were not near Exchange Spire.

They were inside it.

That had not been accidental.

Torlan preferred proximity.

The consulting suite occupied a modest tenant wing two levels below one of the Spire's central administrative sectors, the sort of office space no one prestigious noticed and no one suspicious remembered.

Perfect.

From the corridor entrance the suite looked almost aggressively ordinary.

Which made it useful.

A front reception desk sat just inside the glass frontage.

Beyond it stretched a surprisingly large suite of connected rooms:

side offices for analysts and visiting consultants,

a broad central conference room,

records storage rooms in the rear,

narrow linking corridors,

and more work rooms than a two-person consultancy could reasonably justify.

Alexa noticed immediately.

"This is larger than we need."

Torlan set down his case.

"For now."

She looked at him.

That answered more than it should have.

She walked the suite once in silence, opening doors, checking sight lines.

Then said,

"It looks exactly like a place no one would remember entering."

"Good."

She moved toward the rear window wall.

But the view did not look out toward Exchange Spire—

it looked deeper into it.

An interior atrium opened several levels below, crossed by glass walkways and freight lifts moving in measured patterns. Office lights glowed beyond layered balconies. Departments connected by enclosed bridges disappeared into other sections of the structure.

The building seemed almost alive with order.

Alexa folded her arms.

"We have not rented a front-row seat to the machine."

Torlan stepped beside her.

"No."

She studied the movement below.

"We're already inside it."

That, too, had been intentional.

The larger suite pleased Torlan for another reason.

It had more rooms than they needed now.

Which meant that someday, if needed, it might hold more than two people.

He said none of that aloud.

Not yet.

"Observation begins," he said.

But not immediately.

Because before investigation came something simpler:

learning how to belong.

For two days they did almost nothing suspicious.

Which was deliberate.

They settled.

Opened the office.

Met neighboring tenants.

Asked harmless questions.

Filed dull paperwork.

Became forgettable.

Torlan considered invisibility an art.

Alexa considered it slow.

On the third afternoon, they entered deeper sections of Exchange Spire as if they had every reason to be there.

Which, under their cover, they did.

Its interior impressed even Torlan.

Massive central atriums rose through several levels. Suspended transit platforms moved between departments. Financial exchanges operated behind transparent walls where streams of numbers moved like weather.

It felt less like commerce.

More like organized force.

Alexa stopped near one overlook.

"I may dislike this place."

"Already?"

"It has ambition."

"You say that as criticism."

"Often it is."

They moved deeper.

Observed.

Asked little.

Watched much.

And it was there Torlan first noticed something odd.

Conversations altered around certain people.

Subtle.

Almost invisible.

But altered.

Voices lowered.

Discussions shortened.

People straightened.

One man stepped aside from a corridor as though yielding to a current.

Torlan filed it away.

Fear leaves posture before words.

He had learned that long ago.

Then—

without warning—

Alexa lightly touched his sleeve.

He followed her glance.

Across an upper mezzanine,

walking with no visible hurry—

was a man neither dramatic nor physically imposing.

Medium height.

Dark suit.

Precise movements.

No wasted gestures.

He carried no visible authority.

Yet the corridor seemed to acknowledge him.

Without trying to.

Without choice.

Torlan watched.

"So," Alexa murmured.

"So."

"Kessler?"

Torlan nodded once.

Probably.

They stood still as he passed.

Kessler never looked toward them.

Which somehow made the moment stranger.

He disappeared around a far turn.

Only then did Alexa exhale.

"Well."

Torlan almost smiled.

"You use that word often."

"It means I have run out of better ones."

They resumed walking.

But something had changed.

Names on files had become a person.

And somehow—

more dangerous.

Later, back in the office, Alexa stood looking over the interior atrium lights.

"Did you notice," she said, "no one smiled around him?"

Torlan looked up from notes.

"Yes."

"And no one interrupted him."

"Yes."

"And everyone moved as though already corrected."

Torlan set down his pen.

"Fear often disguises itself as efficiency."

Alexa turned from the window.

That one stayed with her.

"Do you think he saw us?"

Torlan considered.

"No."

Then added:

"But I think we saw enough."

She leaned against the desk.

"What exactly did we see?"

Torlan looked toward the layered reaches of the Spire.

Its hidden floors.

Its immense ordered machinery.

At last he said,

"A system that behaves like it is used to obedience."

Alexa was quiet.

Then:

"That sounds unpleasant."

"Yes."

She studied him.

"You look almost pleased."

"I'm interested."

"That is not much better."

Outside the atrium lights deepened into evening.

Traffic moved in silent currents.

Profitthorn glittered.

Beautiful.

Controlled.

Possibly dangerous.

And for the first time since arriving—

Torlan had the faintest sensation they had not merely entered a trade hub.

They had stepped deeper inside something built to conceal itself.

He looked again into the layered structure of Exchange Spire.

Then said quietly,

"We may have found the machine."

Alexa folded her arms.

"Or the machine may have found us."

Torlan looked at her.

That possibility had occurred to him too.

Neither said it aloud again.

But it remained in the room after the lights came on.

Waiting.

## Chapter 4 - Exchange Spire

By the end of their first week, Torlan had decided Exchange Spire was designed to exhaust curiosity.

That, he suspected, was not accidental.

The place overwhelmed by abundance.

Too many corridors.

Too many departments.

Too much ordinary activity.

If secrets lived here, they did not hide behind locked doors.

They drowned in routine.

Which was often safer.

He and Alexa had developed a pattern.

Morning in their office.

Midday among the Spire's lower commercial divisions.

Afternoons asking harmless questions disguised as consulting curiosity.

Evenings comparing what people had not said.

Increasingly, that last category interested Torlan most.

It was remarkable how much silence could reveal.

On the eighth morning Alexa was reviewing tenant directories when she frowned at a screen.

Torlan noticed.

"That expression usually means trouble."

"It means inconsistency."

"With you that is often the same thing."

She ignored that.

"Three firms occupying linked offices on level seventeen."

"So?"

"They exist."

"That is usually helpful in a business."

"They exist," she repeated, "without behaving as though they need to."

Torlan came around the desk.

She enlarged the records.

Three companies.

Different names.

Different registrations.

Nearly identical financial rhythms.

The kind of thing that made Alexa suspicious on principle.

"Shell structures?"

"Maybe."

He studied them.

Or maybe something arranged to appear ordinary.

Again.

Patterns.

Always patterns.

Alexa looked at him.

"You're doing that."

"What?"

"Admiring architecture."

"I am not admiring it."

"You're close."

He let that pass.

"Let's go look."

By midday they were inside the level seventeen tenant sector.

Quiet.

Too quiet for a commercial floor.

The carpeting thicker.

Voices softer.

Doors more often closed.

Even the lighting seemed to encourage discretion.

Alexa noticed first.

"This floor whispers."

Torlan almost smiled.

"That may be your most alarming sentence this week."

She lowered her voice.

"I'm serious."

"So am I."

They passed reception desks staffed by people too polished to be clerks and too guarded to be casual.

No one was rude.

No one was welcoming.

An art in itself.

Torlan asked one harmless question about trade routing compliance.

The answer came quickly.

Perfectly.

And ended before conversation could begin.

Back in the corridor Alexa said quietly,

"No one here wants accidental dialogue."

"No."

"That bothers me."

"It should."

As they turned a corner, a young records runner carrying folders nearly collided with them.

The man stopped abruptly.

Apologized too quickly.

And glanced—not at them—

but down the corridor behind them.

Toward a security camera.

Then hurried away.

Alexa watched him go.

"Well."

Torlan looked at her.

"You're using that word more."

"I have earned it."

They continued.

Near an atrium overlook they stopped beside a public information terminal.

Torlan pretended to study freight statistics.

Actually he was watching people.

A habit Marcus claimed made him unsettling at parties.

Three employees crossed the floor.

Conversation ceased when a fourth approached.

Instantly.

Not naturally.

Conditioned.

Fear leaves seams.

And he was beginning to see them.

That afternoon, in a cafeteria designed to look casual and somehow succeeding only partially, Alexa stirred coffee she had no intention of drinking.

"What do you make of it?"

Torlan considered.

"Kessler may not rule by visible pressure."

She waited.

"He may rule by anticipated correction."

Alexa looked up.

That landed.

"That sounds worse."

"It often is."

She leaned back.

"Can I ask something unpleasant?"

"You often do."

"What if we're wrong?"

He looked at her.

"About Kessler?"

"Yes."

"That he's merely severe.
Merely efficient.
Merely unpleasant."

Torlan was quiet a moment.

Then:

"Fear does not gather around ordinary managers."

She nodded slowly.

That was Fair.

Later that day they saw Kessler again.

Briefly.

A corridor crossing.

Nothing more.

Yet as he passed, two senior administrators changed direction to let him through.

Not deferentially.

Reflexively.

That interested Torlan more than overt fear would have.

Power most secure is often the least announced.

Alexa watched Kessler disappear.

Then said,

"I still have not seen anyone disagree with him."

"Neither have I."

"That may be impossible."

"Or expensive."

She looked at him sideways.

"That was bleak."

"Accurate."

Back at their office that evening they spread notes across the conference table.

What they had gathered was almost embarrassingly small.

No evidence.

No smoking system.

No exposed crime.

Only impressions.

Patterns.

Silences.

And yet something coherent was forming.

Alexa pointed at three names she had marked.

"These employees all transferred after internal disputes."

"Disputes?"

"Officially."

"Meaning?"

She looked up.

"Meaning records say dispute.

Faces say fear."

Torlan nodded.

"Can we speak to any?"

"Current employees?"

She shook her head.

"They won't talk."

That came quickly enough to matter.

He noticed.

"You're sure."

"Yes."

"How?"

Alexa gave a faint smile.

"Because they've already refused."

He blinked.

"When?"

"This afternoon."

"You didn't mention it."

"I wanted to see if you noticed the pattern first."

Torlan stared.

"That is a manipulative research method."

"Effective?"

Annoyingly—

yes.

He accepted it.

After a pause he said,

"Then current employees are closed."

Alexa nodded.

"For now."

Torlan walked toward the rear window.

Looked out over the interior atrium.

Lights glowed through layered levels.

Departments still active.

Movement everywhere.

And hidden within it—

somewhere—

Kessler.

Marcus's words came back unexpectedly:

*Do not admire him.*

Torlan disliked remembering that now.

Because he understood the warning.

Systems like this could fascinate.

Dangerously.

Alexa spoke behind him.

"So what next?"

He did not turn.

"People who still work for Kessler fear him."

"Yes."

"People who no longer work for him may not."

She understood at once.

Former employees.

Discharged staff.

Those who survived.

At last, the next door appeared.

Alexa gathered her notes.

"I can begin finding them."

Torlan nodded.

Then quietly:

"We stop looking at the machine."

She looked up.

"And?"

"We ask the people caught inside it."

That sat in the room.

Right.

Necessary.

And riskier.

Alexa smiled faintly.

"Now we're getting somewhere."

Torlan kept looking into the lit depths of Exchange Spire.

Perhaps.

Or perhaps—

he thought but did not say—

they were merely approaching the point where the machine noticed questions.

He almost preferred not knowing.

Almost.

At the door Alexa paused.

"One more thing."

He turned.

"What?"

She pointed at his notes.

"You have written Kessler's name six times in the margin."

He looked down.

She was right.

"And?"

She gave him a look.

"That is either investigation…

or obsession."

Then she left him with that.

Torlan looked once more toward the glowing atrium.

And for the first time since arriving—

he wondered whether studying the architect was slowly becoming a way of being studied.

That thought stayed longer than he liked.

And when he finally turned off the office lights—
it came with him.

## Chapter 5 - Quiet Irregularities

Former employees proved harder to find than Alexa expected.

That alone interested Torlan.

In ordinary commerce, dismissed people often liked to talk.

Sometimes too much.

Here—

they disappeared.

Or seemed to.

Records ended.

Forwarding contacts failed.

Consulting licenses quietly lapsed.

Some had left Profitthorn altogether.

A few, Alexa suspected, had chosen to become difficult to find.

Which was not the same as lost.

By the fourth day she had assembled a list.

Short.

Cautious.

Promising.

She slid it across the conference table.

Torlan looked at the names.

"Only seven?"

"Seven willing to be located."

He looked up.

"That is a disturbing phrase."

"Yes."

He read down the list.

Former auditors.

Two compliance officers.

One regional operations manager.

A logistics reviewer.

And one name circled twice.

Deren Mall.

Alexa noticed him pause.

"That one interests me."

"Why?"

"Discharged eight years ago."

"Long time."

"Still living quietly under a consulting license he barely uses."

Torlan nodded.

"A man avoiding visibility."

"Or preserving it."

By noon they were seated in a narrow café three levels removed from Exchange Spire, waiting for Deren Mall.

The café had chosen privacy over fashion decades ago and never regretted it.

Good coffee.

Bad chairs.

Excellent discretion.

Marcus would have approved.

Deren arrived ten minutes late.

Which, Torlan suspected, was deliberate.

He was older than records suggested.

Careful-faced.

Not timid.

Careful.

Different thing.

He sat without greeting.

Studied both of them.

Then said,

"You are not trade consultants."

Alexa answered before Torlan could.

"Neither are you."

That surprised him enough to almost smile.

Almost.

Good.

He leaned back.

"Who sent you?"

"No one."

That earned skepticism.

Torlan spoke.

"We have questions about Exchange Spire."

Deren looked toward the windows.

Then back.

"I do not."

Interesting answer.

Torlan let silence work.

Eventually Deren sighed.

"I used to."

There it was.

The first crack.

Conversation came slowly.

Never in dramatic revelations.

In fragments.

Corrections.

Half-finished warnings.

More believable that way.

Life under Kessler, Deren explained, was orderly—until one asked the wrong question.

Then order changed shape.

Alexa asked,

"What wrong question?"

Deren stirred coffee he never drank.

"Any question implying a record may be wrong."

Torlan said,

"And if someone asks anyway?"

Deren met his eyes.

"They stop advancing."

A pause.

"Sometimes stop remaining."

Alexa held that quietly.

Not dramatic.

Worse.

Matter-of-fact.

Torlan asked,

"Was Kessler directly involved?"

Deren gave a strange look.

"You still think in direct involvement."

He leaned closer.

"That is not how power like his works."

That line lodged deep.

They left two hours later with almost no evidence.

And much more concern.

Outside, Alexa walked several steps before speaking.

"Well."

Torlan looked at her.

"Again?"

"It remains useful."

She looked back toward the café.

"He was afraid."

"Yes."

"Years later."

"Yes."

She frowned.

"That bothers me."

"It should."

Over the next week they met three more former employees.

Patterns emerged.

Different stories.

Same atmosphere.

Control.

Correction.

Fear.

No one accused Kessler of crimes outright.

Curiously—

that made the accounts feel truer.

People with rehearsed grievances often exaggerate.

These people minimized.

That interested Torlan more.

One former reviewer said:

"Kessler never threatens.

He lets consequences introduce themselves."

Alexa wrote that down immediately.

Another said:

"No one crosses him twice."

Torlan wrote that one down.

But the fifth interview changed things.

Because this one came with anger.

And scars.

His name was Renn Voss.

Former senior analyst.

Dismissed under fraud allegations later dropped.

He laughed once when Alexa asked what Kessler was like.

Not kindly.

"You think Kessler controls people?"

He leaned forward.

"Kessler trains people to control themselves."

Even Torlan went still at that.

Afterward Alexa said quietly,

"That may be the truest thing anyone has said."

He agreed.

That night in the office they spread notes across the large conference table.

Fragments.

Warnings.

No proof.

Yet something darker than evidence was accumulating.

A culture.

And cultures can convict.

If understood.

Alexa tapped one pattern emerging through personnel histories.

"See this?"

Repeated names surfaced.

Employees who questioned routing anomalies.

Transfers.

Dismissals.

Disappearances from the system.

Torlan studied it.

Then said,

"It behaves like filtration."

Alexa looked up.

"Yes."

Undesirable particles removed.

The phrase chilled even as he said it.

She leaned back.

"You know what troubles me?"

"What?"

"Kessler may believe this is ethical."

Torlan considered.

"That may be the worst possibility."

A long silence.

Then Alexa pulled another file.

One name.

Older.

Different.

Flagged repeatedly.

Garron Vale.

Torlan read.

Former executive-level accounting officer.

Convicted.

Twenty-year sentence.

He frowned.

"Accounting."

"Yes."

That mattered.

A lot.

More than the others.

Because this was not dismissal.

This was burial.

Alexa slid a prison transfer record across.

"He asked questions."

"And paid for it."

Possibly.

Torlan read further.

Something in the case felt wrong.

Too complete.

Too clean.

Manufactured certainty often has a smell.

This had it.

He looked up.

"This may be different."

Alexa nodded.

"I think so."

She hesitated.

Then:

"There's one more thing."

He waited.

She pointed to a note from a former employee.

Single sentence.

Underlined.

**If anyone knew where the hidden books were, it would have been Garron.**

Torlan read it twice.

Hidden books.

Not records.

Not files.

Books.

Alexa watched him thinking.

"You're doing it again."

"What?"

"Admiring architecture."

He almost smiled.

"No."

This time she wasn't convinced.

He stood and walked toward the atrium window.

Lights below moved in silent channels.

The machine again.

Always the machine.

But now—

perhaps—

someone inside it had once tried to resist.

That changed things substantially.

Alexa came beside him.

"Prison?"

"Yes."

She studied him.

She nodded once, as if that were entirely reasonable.

Then asked quietly

"Do you think Garron was framed?"

Torlan looked into the layered lights of Exchange Spire.

After a long pause:

"I think," he said,

"we may have found the first man who tried to stop Kessler."

That sat between them.

It sat between them, heavy and almost solemn.

At last Alexa said,

"If that's true…"

He looked at her.

"Yes?"

She finished softly,

"…then this may be larger than exposure."

He understood.

Larger than exposing corruption.

Potentially—

righting an injustice.

A different mission—deeper than exposure.

That mattered. Deeply.

Torlan gathered the Garron file.

Closed it.

Decision made.

Tomorrow they would visit a prison.

And perhaps—

for the first time—

hear the machine described from inside.

As he turned out the lights that night, one thought lingered.

Not about Kessler.

Not even about Garron.

But about something one frightened former employee had said hours earlier:

*Kessler never threatens.*

*He lets consequences introduce themselves.*

Torlan suspected they had just been introduced.

## Chapter 6 - Garron Vale

The prison lay outside Profitthorn's trade perimeter, where commerce thinned and architecture became practical.

No polished towers.

No mirrored facades.

No ambition pretending to be beauty.

Only walls.

Security fields.

Steel.

Necessary ugliness.

Alexa studied the complex through the transport window.

"It looks cheerful."

Torlan glanced at her.

"That was almost optimism."

"It was sarcasm."

"Good. I was concerned."

She looked back at the prison.

"I dislike places built entirely around the assumption people fail."

Torlan considered that.

"Some institutions are."

"And some?"

"Are built because others do."

That earned him a look.

"You're philosophical again."

He accepted the charge.

The intake process was slow.

Intentionally so.

Forms checked twice.

Identity verified three times.

Permissions questioned as though truth might change under repetition.

Marcus would have hated it.

Eventually they were led into a visitation chamber with plain walls and old furniture that had surrendered all ambition years earlier.

Nothing here asked to be admired.

That too felt honest.

They waited.

Alexa sat quietly.

Torlan reviewed the file again.

Garron Vale.

Year three of a twenty-year sentence.

Financial misconduct.

Asset concealment.

Fraud conspiracy.

The charges still felt too neat.

Like an equation balanced for display.

The door opened.

Garron entered.

And somehow was not what Torlan expected.

Not broken.

Not hardened.

Worn. There is a difference.

He moved with a quiet dignity difficult to fake.

Older than his file image.

Greyer.

Thinner.

But composed—remarkably composed.

His eyes went first to Alexa.

Then Torlan.

Then the file.

And he smiled faintly.

"You brought paperwork."

Torlan stood.

"We thought it respectful."

Garron sat.

"Then you are not from around here."

Alexa nearly smiled.

Good.

That helped.

For a few moments conversation stayed careful.

Ordinary.

Testing.

Then Garron looked at Torlan.

"You did not come to ask whether I'm innocent."

No point pretending.

Torlan answered directly.

"No."

Garron nodded.

"Good."

He leaned back.

"You came to ask about Kessler."

Not a question.

Alexa noticed.

"You expected that?"

Garron gave a small tired smile.

"I've expected it for three years."

That landed.

Torlan asked quietly,

"Why?"

"Because machines eventually consume enough people that someone begins tracing gears."

There was that word again.

Machine.

Torlan opened the file but did not look at it.

"We have spoken with former employees."

Garron nodded once.

"The frightened ones."

"Yes."

He folded his hands.

"They likely told you Kessler is dangerous."

"In different words."

"They were being polite."

Silence followed.

Not uncomfortable.

Heavy.

Then Torlan asked,

"What happened to you?"

Garron did not answer immediately.

When he did, his voice was calm.

Almost too calm.

"I asked questions."

Alexa said softly,

"About accounts?"

"Yes."

"Questionable transfers?"

"Yes."

"Hidden routing structures?"

Garron looked at her carefully.

"You've seen traces."

"Some."

He nodded.

Then said,

"I thought truth would protect me."

No self-pity.

Which made it hit harder.

He looked at Torlan.

"Do not make that mistake."

Torlan let that sit.

Then:

"You tried reporting what you found."

"Yes."

"And?"

Garron gave a hollow little laugh.

"My lawyer belonged to Kessler.

My judge owed Kessler.

My evidence vanished.

My questions became motive."

Alexa stopped writing.

Even she needed a moment.

Torlan asked,

"You believe you were framed."

Garron looked directly at him.

"No."

Pause.

"I know."

That hung in the room.

Solid as stone.

After a while Alexa asked,

"Your family?"

Something softened.

First real shift in Garron.

"My wife visits every month."

He looked down once.

Then up.

"She tells me the children still say we are waiting.

Not serving.

Waiting."

Torlan felt that.

Deeply.

Garron added quietly,

"They never doubted me."

No one spoke for several seconds.

Some things should breathe.

Then Torlan said,

"We think Kessler may sit atop something larger."

Garron studied him.

Then nodded.

"Now we arrive."

He leaned closer.

"You think Kessler runs corruption."

Another pause.

"Kessler curates it."

Wonderful word.

Chilling word.

Alexa wrote it down instantly.

Torlan asked,

"Can he be exposed?"

Garron gave him a long look.

Then shook his head.

"Not exposed."

The word seemed dismissed.

"Then how?"

A longer silence.

Garron almost seemed weighing whether to say it.

Then:

"Trap him."

There it was.

Not fully born yet, but there.

First breath of the sting.

Torlan did not move.

Neither did Alexa.

Garron continued.

"Kessler survives accusation.

He anticipates investigation.

He survives honesty."

He leaned in.

"But men who believe they control outcomes…"

He stopped.

Torlan finished quietly.

"…can be made to step into one."

Garron smiled faintly.

Now he was studying Torlan.

"You have thought dangerous thoughts."

"Occasionally."

Alexa muttered,

"More than occasionally."

Garron almost laughed.

First warmth of the meeting.

Then he said something that shifted everything.

"If anyone can bury Kessler…"

he lowered his voice,

"…it begins with the books."

Torlan looked up sharply.

Books.

Again.

Not records.

Books.

Very deliberate.

"What books?"

Garron hesitated.

Then shook his head.

"Too much for today."

Frustrating.

But believable.

He pointed lightly at the file.

"Read my conviction records again.

Not the charges.

The omissions."

Then:

"There are ledgers Kessler trusts more than systems."

That line lodged deep.

Alexa asked,

"Where?"

Garron gave a small smile.

"If I tell you that now…"

He let it hang.

That was Fair.

The visit ended too soon.

A guard appeared.

Time called.

But something important had already happened.

As Garron stood to leave, Torlan said,

"We may return."

Garron nodded.

"You should."

Then, almost as afterthought:

"And when you do…"

he looked at both of them,

"come prepared to think like thieves."

And then he was gone.

The door closed.

Alexa sat motionless.

Then:

"Well."

Torlan laughed once, actual laughter—rare enough to matter.

Outside, walking toward transport, neither spoke for some time.

Finally Alexa said,

"Curates corruption."

Torlan nodded.

"That will stay with me."

She looked at him.

"Trap him."

"Yes."

"Books."

"Yes."

She stopped walking.

"You realize this may no longer be research."

Torlan looked back at the prison walls.

"I know."

She lowered her voice.

"I think Garron may have just handed us the beginning of a sting."

Torlan said nothing.

Because she was right.

And both knew it.

As the transport lifted back toward Profitthorn, Exchange Spire appeared again on the horizon.

Silver.

Distant.

Patient.

Torlan looked at it and thought not of architecture this time—

but of ledgers hidden somewhere inside it.

And of a prisoner who had said:

*Come prepared to think like thieves.*

That did not feel like warning.

It felt less like warning

and more like invitation.

And that was somehow more dangerous.

## Chapter 7 - First Theory of the Sting

They returned from the prison carrying almost nothing.

No documents.

No names they could prove.

No evidence admissible anywhere.

And yet Torlan felt as though they had brought back something far heavier.

A possibility.

Sometimes possibilities weigh more than facts.

That evening the office lights burned later than usual.

The conference room—oversized for a consulting firm and increasingly useful for other things—held files spread in widening circles across the table.

Garron's case notes.

Former employee interviews.

Trade maps.

Ownership diagrams.

And, written alone in the center of one page in Alexa's handwriting:

**Trap him.**

Torlan had been staring at those words too long.

Alexa noticed.

"You've read those two words at least twenty times."

"Twenty-three."

"That is not reassuring."

"No."

She leaned back in her chair.

The atrium lights beyond the rear windows had thinned into nighttime traffic.

Exchange Spire seemed quieter after dark.

Which somehow made it feel more watchful.

Torlan said at last,

"Exposure will not work."

Alexa nodded immediately.

She had already reached that conclusion.

"Too protected."

"Yes."

"Too distributed."

"Yes."

"Too intelligent."

He looked at her.

"That as well."

Silence.

Then she said it.

"Say it."

Torlan did not pretend not to understand.

"The only way through this may be to force Kessler into exposing himself."

Alexa folded her arms.

"There it is."

He gave her a look.

"What?"

"The dangerous thought."

She was not wrong.

Torlan stood and began pacing slowly around the conference room.

A habit he denied having.

Alexa never let him deny it successfully.

"He survives accusation," he said.

"Garron was clear."

"Yes."

"He survives investigation."

"Yes."

"He may even survive evidence."

Alexa frowned.

That was harder.

But perhaps true.

Then Torlan stopped pacing.

Which usually meant he had arrived somewhere.

"What if," he said slowly,

"we stop trying to prove Kessler guilty…"

Alexa waited.

…and make Kessler help prove it."

The room became very still.

That sentence had weight.

Alexa sat forward.

"That sounds disturbingly like a sting."

Torlan did not answer.

Which was answer enough.

She looked almost amused.

"You realize this is the part reasonable people leave the room."

"We have not been reasonable for some time."

She stood and moved to the board at the far wall.

Picked up a marker.

Wrote:

KESSLER

Then circled it.

Below it:

HOW TO FORCE ERROR?

She turned.

"Suppose we indulge this."

Torlan almost smiled.

"You make dangerous thoughts sound academic."

"That is how dangerous thoughts survive."

She pointed.

"How do you force a man like Kessler to make a mistake?"

Torlan considered.

"You do not force error."

He walked to the board.

Took the marker.

"You force decision."

He wrote beneath hers:

FORCE DECISION.

Alexa read it.

And nodded slowly.

They worked for hours.

Not planning a sting.

Not yet.

Only testing whether such a thing could exist.

They discarded possibilities almost as fast as they raised them.

Public exposure.

Too weak.

Regulatory audit.

Too corruptible.

Leak evidence.

Too easy for Kessler to bury.

Every route bent back to the same problem.

Kessler anticipated frontal attacks.

Garron had been right.

Eventually Alexa sat down again.

Exhausted.

And said,

"What if we are asking the wrong question?"

Torlan looked up.

"What should we ask?"

Not how to accuse him."

She let that settle.

"How to make him trust the wrong move."

Torlan stared.

That was good.

He said quietly,

"That is not accusation."

"No."

"That is entrapment."

She smiled faintly.

"There is a less alarming word?"

"Not currently."

They both laughed.

A little.

Needed.

Then Torlan grew serious again.

"Kessler trusts systems."

"Yes."

"Processes."

"Yes."

"Control."

Alexa looked at him.

"And himself."

That mattered enormously.

He wrote one new word on the board:

CONTROL.

Circled it.

Then:

USE CONTROL AGAINST HIM

Neither spoke for a while.

Because now—

for the first time—

the thing felt conceivable.

Dangerously conceivable.

Alexa looked toward the darkened atrium.

"I think we are inventing trouble."

Torlan answered,

"Yes."

Then:

"Possibly the useful kind."

Near midnight Alexa was reviewing Garron's conviction file again when she stopped.

"There is something odd."

Torlan came over.

She tapped the page.

"See this?"

He did.

Accounting signatory authority.

Special access designation.

Restricted ledger privileges.

He frowned.

"Garron once sat close to the center."

"Yes."

Close enough to know where books might exist.

Close enough perhaps to know who keeps them.

Alexa looked up.

"What are you thinking?"

Torlan said it slowly.

"If hidden ledgers exist…"

"Yes?"

"They may be the lever."

That changed the room again.

Because suddenly the sting had object.

Not abstract strategy.

Target.

Leverage.

Possibility.

Alexa whispered,

"Oh."

Torlan looked at her.

"What?"

"I think…"

she leaned back,

"…this may actually work."

He was not ready to say that.

But he was beginning to fear it might.

Which was oddly similar.

After a long silence Alexa said,

"We need more people."

He looked at her.

"Yes."

That admission mattered.

Because until then the idea had belonged to two minds.

Now it demanded a team.

Resources.

Roles.

Structure.

Something larger.

Which made it real.

Torlan sat again.

For a long time neither spoke.

Only studied the notes.

The board.

The dangerous little architecture growing among scraps of thought.

At last Alexa said,

"What do we call this?"

Torlan looked up.

"This?"

She gestured at the board.

At the impossible beginning.

"Yes."

He considered.

Then:

"A first theory."

"Of?"

He looked toward the circled name.

KESSLER.

Then back.

"A sting."

Alexa smiled.

Not because it was amusing.

Because she recognized the moment.

The instant a plan stops being speculation.

And begins becoming destiny.

At the office door she paused before leaving.

"One concern."

He waited.

"What if Kessler is better at strategy than we are?"

Torlan thought.

It was a fair question.

Then said quietly:

"Then we had better become better."

She gave a faint nod, apparently satisfied.

Then she left.

Torlan remained alone in the conference room.

Board still lit.

Words still visible:

Trap him.

Force decision.

Use control against him.

He stared at them a long while.

Then added one final note at the bottom.

Not for Alexa.

For himself.

He wrote:

MAKE KESSLER THE MARK.

He set the marker down.

And for the first time—

the name of a game not yet played had entered the room.

Outside, somewhere in the layered machinery of Exchange Spire, lights still burned in unseen offices.

Kessler perhaps among them.

Unaware.

For now.

Torlan looked once more at the board.

Then switched off the lights.

And carried the first shape of the sting home with him.

## Chapter 8 - Pressure Builds

Ideas had weight.

Torlan was discovering that some had gravity.

The sting had begun as theory.

By the third day it behaved more like responsibility.

Which was more dangerous.

The conference room no longer resembled a consulting office at all.

Maps covered one wall.

Financial diagrams another.

Questions multiplied faster than answers.

And in the center of it all—

the board remained.

Trap him.

Force decision.

Use control against him.

Make Kessler the mark.

Alexa had begun calling it, with a straight face she did not entirely deserve,

"the wall of increasingly questionable life choices."

Torlan had not objected.

Mostly because it was accurate.

They spent the morning attempting something disappointing.

To prove the sting unnecessary.

Torlan insisted on it.

Any dangerous strategy worth considering should survive attempts to avoid it.

So they tested alternatives again.

Expose through regulators.

Dead end.

Use former employees.

Too weak.

Appeal through courts.

Possibly suicidal.

Leak partial evidence.

Likely warns Kessler.

Every road curved back.

To the same hard center.

No simple exposure.

No clean legal route.

No ordinary rescue for Garron.

By midday Alexa dropped a file onto the table.

Harder than necessary.

"That is the seventh elegant failure today."

Torlan looked up.

"Only seventh?"

"You missed two."

He almost smiled.

Then she leaned forward.

"I think we need to admit something."

He waited.

She tapped the board.

"This may be the only path left."

He knew.

He had known.

Hearing it aloud changed things.

The room felt quieter after.

As if decisions sometimes make sound when they settle.

Torlan walked to the rear window.

The interior atrium below moved in ordered currents.

People carrying reports.

Freight lifts rising.

Systems turning.

Always turning.

"The machine depends on predictable motion," he said.

Alexa looked up.

"Yes."

"What if disruption comes disguised as routine?"

That made her sit straighter.

"Say that again."

He turned.

"If a sting works…"

he said slowly,

"it may have to hide inside ordinary process."

Alexa stared.

Then smiled.

"That is unpleasantly clever."

He accepted this as criticism.

Barely.

She stood.

Walked to the board.

Added a new line:

HIDE THE STING INSIDE ROUTINE

She stepped back.

The board was beginning to look alarming.

A good sign—perhaps.

That afternoon they reviewed one difficult truth neither had wanted to say.

Two people were not enough.

At last Alexa said it.

"We need others."

Torlan nodded.

No resistance.

Because he had already arrived there.

"Specialists," he said.

"Different roles."

"Separate strengths."

Alexa folded her arms.

"And people you trust."

That mattered most.

He looked around the unexpectedly large office.

Its extra rooms.

Unused desks.

Silent corridors.

Earlier choices suddenly looked prophetic.

Alexa noticed where his gaze went.

"Oh no."

He looked at her.

"What?"

"You're imagining filling this place."

"Possibly," he said.

"Yes."

She laughed softly.

"I knew that 'for now' line bothered me."

Torlan said,

"The suite may be useful."

"It may become a conspiracy."

"Operationally."

"Of course."

They spent hours sketching what roles might be needed.

Research.

Surveillance.

Impersonation.

Technical misdirection.

Financial traps.

Each new note made the thing feel both smarter—

and riskier.

At one point Alexa set down her pen.

"You realize if Marcus sees this board he'll call it madness."

"He may be correct."

She considered.

"Probably."

Late afternoon brought something else.

A reminder.

Pressure was already moving.

While reviewing routine ownership disputes, Alexa froze over one file.

"What?"

She turned screen toward him.

A dispute filing.

Minor.

Routine.

Yet routed unusually fast.

Through channels tied to Kessler.

Torlan studied it.

Then looked up.

"He responds quickly when ownership is threatened."

Alexa's eyes widened slightly.

Authentication pressure.

The first faint shadow of it.

Neither fully understood it yet.

But both felt it.

A lever, perhaps.

She whispered,

"That could matter later."

"Yes."

Another seed planted.

Evening deepened.

Office lights remained on.

The atrium below grew quieter.

The building seemed to lower its voice at night.

At last Alexa leaned back.

"We have a theory."

Torlan nodded.

"We need an operation."

"Yes."

"And to get one…"

She waited.

Torlan finished:

"We call the others."

That line changed the room.

Because saying it made it real.

No longer private speculation.

Now expansion.

Commitment.

There was no walking backward from summoning allies.

Alexa looked almost solemn.

"When?"

Torlan checked the clock.

Then:

"Tonight."

That surprised even her.

"You've already decided."

"Yes."

"You keep doing that."

He accepted the charge.

He moved to the secure terminal.

Paused.

Not typing yet.

Thinking.

Because messages like this altered trajectories.

Marcus.

Dooley.

The others.

Once sent—

the game widened.

Alexa watched.

Then asked quietly,

"What do you tell them?"

Torlan thought.

Then:

"Come separately."

She nodded.

"No patterns."

"No cluster arrivals."

"No one knows who arrives when."

The sting was already shaping its own rules.

Torlan began composing.

Brief.

Encrypted.

Simple.

Need assistance.

Travel separately.

Stagger arrivals.

Use cover routes.

Await further instructions.

No explanation.

The kind of message trusted people understand instantly.

His hand paused over send.

Alexa looked at him.

Second thoughts?"

"No."

"Then why pause?"

Torlan said quietly,

"Because this may be the moment the idea becomes dangerous."

Alexa smiled faintly.

"I believe that was several chapters ago."

He sent it.

Just like that.

A soft confirmation light appeared.

Nothing dramatic.

No alarms.

No music.

Only a message gone outward.

Yet both felt something shift.

Like a door quietly opening.

For a long while neither spoke.

Then Alexa looked at the board.

At all those dangerous thoughts.

And said,

"Well."

Torlan looked over.

"That word again."

"It remains useful."

She gathered her notes.

Stopped at the door.

Turned.

"One prediction."

He waited.

"This office is about to become much less quiet."

He looked at the empty side rooms.

The oversized conference room.

The unused corridors.

Perhaps.

After she left, Torlan remained alone.

The secure terminal dimmed.

The board remained lit on the wall.

Exchange Spire breathed beyond the glass.

Somewhere above, perhaps only floors away,

Kessler continued in perfect confidence.

Unaware.

For now.

Torlan stepped to the window.

Looked into the layered machinery.

And thought of Garron's words.

*Come prepared to think like thieves.*
He understood now.
The invitation had been accepted.
Quietly.
Fully.
And somewhere beyond Profitthorn,
trusted friends had just begun traveling toward a sting.
The storm was no longer gathering.
It had begun.

## Chapter 9 - The Honest Officer

A week before the others were due to begin arriving, Torlan raised a problem neither he nor Alexa had yet said aloud.

It happened over coffee.

Which was fitting.

Most dangerous thoughts in their partnership seemed to begin over coffee.

Alexa was reviewing old enforcement records while Torlan stared absently at the interior atrium below.

Then he said,

"We have overlooked something."

Alexa did not look up.

"That is rarely encouraging."

"If the sting works—"

She looked up immediately.

"When."

He accepted the correction.

"When the sting works…"

he turned toward her,

"…who receives the evidence?"

Silence.

Then Alexa set down her cup.

Because that was a very real question.

And a very serious one.

Corruption this deep did not end because ledgers appeared.

Not if handed to corrupt officials.

Not if buried.

Not if misfiled.

Truth required somewhere to land.

Alexa said quietly,

"That is not a small problem."

"No."

In fact, it might be fatal.

For the next two days they looked not for criminals.

But for one honest man.

Strangely, that proved harder.

Police names surfaced tangled in compromise.

Internal affairs complaints vanished.

Cases dissolved.

Judges dismissed things too quickly.

Too many doors bent.

Until one name kept appearing where buried things resisted burial.

Chief Inspector Arlen Doss.

Again.

And again.

Never celebrated.

Never promoted much.

Never politically favored.

But always present at the edge of inconvenient investigations.

Torlan tapped one old report.

"He pushed Kessler once."

Alexa nodded.

"And was pushed back."

Interesting.

Very.

She looked up.

"Do we approach him?"

Torlan considered.

Carefully.

"If he is honest—"

"Yes?"

"He may distrust strangers more than criminals."

Alexa smiled faintly.

"That sounds promising."

They arranged no official meeting.

Nothing recorded.

Nothing traceable.

Three days later they found Doss exactly where a man like him perhaps should be found—

not in headquarters.

In archives.

Reading reports.

Of course.

The records annex was nearly empty at that hour.

Tall shelves.

Muted lights.

Dust that had survived administrative reform.

Doss stood at a high table reviewing a file as though the world were most understandable line by line.

Mid-fifties perhaps.

Weathered face.

Immaculate uniform.

Sharp eyes that missed almost nothing.

He looked up once as they approached.

And somehow managed to seem unsurprised and suspicious at the same time.

Difficult combination.

Torlan respected it instantly.

Doss closed the file.

"You are not here by accident."

Not a question.

Torlan said,

"No."

Doss studied both of them.

Then:

"You rented the consulting offices in Exchange Spire."

Alexa blinked.

"You know that."

"I read occupancy reports."

Of course he did.

That was almost reassuring.

Almost.

Doss gestured toward two chairs.

"Sit."

No hospitality.

No ceremony.

Just precision.

They sat.

For a moment no one spoke.

Then Doss asked:

"Why are two consultants researching officers dismissed for corruption?"

Direct.

Torlan appreciated direct.

"We are studying a man named Kessler."

No visible reaction.

Doss leaned back slightly.

"Many study Kessler."

"Not successfully."

That almost earned the faintest hint of approval.

Almost.

At length Doss said,

"And why bring this to me?"

Torlan answered plainly.

"Because we believe you can be trusted."

Doss looked at him for a long time.

Then said:

"That is either compliment…

or burden."

"Yes."

Alexa nearly smiled.

Doss did not.

Good.

He should not smile easily.

Torlan said,

"We may eventually obtain evidence."

Doss interrupted.

"May?"

"Possibly."

"What kind?"

"We do not yet know."

Doss nodded once.

At last he said quietly:

"You are wise not to tell me what you do not yet possess."

That line mattered.

He understood caution.

Alexa asked,

"You investigated Kessler."

Doss's expression changed almost imperceptibly.

Harder.

"Yes."

"Three times?"

He looked at her sharply.

"You have read old reports."

"Some."

He folded his hands.

"They disappeared."

"The reports?"

"The cases."

A simple answer.

A heavy one.

After a pause he added,

"I knew what I suspected."

He looked down once.

Then back.

"I just couldn't prove it."

There it was.

The line.

Earned.

True.

Silence held.

Then Torlan said what he had really come to ask.

"If we bring you something real…"

Doss watched him.

"…will it survive?"

That seemed to interest him more than anything yet.

A long pause.

Then Doss answered:

"If you bring me truth…"

another pause,

"…I will not let it disappear."

Granite.

Exactly right.

Alexa felt it too.

She leaned forward.

"There may be danger."

Doss gave the faintest trace of dry humor.

"There already is."

Excellent.

Torlan liked him even more.

Doss stood.

Walked to a shelf.

Returned with an old sealed case folder.

Set it down.

Kessler-linked investigations.

Buried.

Suppressed.

Dormant.

He touched the file lightly.

"I have waited years for someone reckless enough to come asking."

Alexa said,

"We prefer determined."

Doss looked at her.

"Call it what lets you sleep."

That nearly made her laugh.

Nearly.

Then Doss became serious again.

He lowered his voice.

"I am not part of whatever you are planning."

Torlan nodded.

"We understand."

Doss continued:

"I ask no details.

I want no names.

I want no methods."

Another pause.

"But if one day you place evidence in my hands…"

he looked at each of them,

"…I will carry it as far as law can carry it."

There.

That was the covenant.

It was quiet, simple, and irrevocable.

Exactly what they needed.

Nothing more.

Nothing less.

They spoke only a little after that.

Enough to establish secure ways to reach him.

Nothing elaborate.

Nothing dramatic.

And that too felt right.

As they stood to leave, Doss said one final thing.

Without looking up from the old file.

"Kessler believes systems fail because men are weak."

He lifted his eyes.

"He has forgotten they can also fail because honest men refuse to move."

Torlan carried that with him.

They both did.

Outside the annex, walking back through the Spire, Alexa was quiet for a long time.

Then finally:

"Well."

Torlan laughed softly.

"Still using that word."

"It continues earning its keep."

She glanced at him.

"You trust him?"

"Yes."

"Completely?"

Torlan thought.

Then:

"As much as one should trust a man who reads archival reports for recreation."

Back at the office, the board still stood waiting.

Dangerous thoughts.

Sting theories.

Half-formed architecture.

But now—

something had changed.

The plan had somewhere to land.

Torlan looked at the words:

Make Kessler the mark.

Then added one line beneath it.

For himself.

For later.

For the day evidence existed.

Deliver truth to Doss.

He set down the marker.

Alexa read it.

And nodded.

No commentary needed.

Outside, the atrium lights glowed.

Exchange Spire breathed in layered silence.

Somewhere above,

Kessler worked in complete confidence.

Still unaware.

For now.

And somewhere inside the same machine—

quietly unnoticed—

stood one honest officer waiting beside old buried cases.

Waiting, perhaps, for truth.

## Chapter 10 - Calling the Others

The messages were brief.

That was deliberate.

Torlan trusted brevity when danger increased.

Especially among friends.

Each message contained only what was necessary:

Come separately.

Stagger arrivals.

Use cover routes.

Await instructions.

No mention of Kessler.

No mention of a sting.

Nothing that could wound them if intercepted.

Yet everyone receiving it would understand one thing immediately.

Torlan was asking for more than help.

He was asking for trust.

And among this group—

that carried weight.

The first reply came from Marcus.

It contained only five words.

**You have found trouble again.**

No greeting.

No question.

No surprise.

Very Marcus.

Alexa read it and said,

“That is almost affectionate.”

“It is profoundly affectionate.”

The second reply came hours later.

Shorter still.

**Understood. Traveling separately.**

Then another.

Then another.

Quiet confirmations blinking across the secure terminal like small lights in distant weather.

One by one—

the team began moving.

And the sting, still half theory, began acquiring people.

Which made it more dangerous.

And much more real.

Torlan stood at the rear window overlooking the atrium after the final confirmation arrived.

Alexa noticed.

“You always look out there when planning turns serious.”

“I do not.”

“You do.”

He let the accusation pass.

“Everyone is coming.”

Alexa folded her arms.

“Yes.”

Then after a pause:

“That is the moment one should perhaps become concerned.”

“Only now?”

She gave him a look.

"More concerned."

Their next challenge was secrecy.

Not merely hiding arrivals—

burying pattern.

The team would not arrive together.

Would not stay together.

Would not even appear connected.

That was essential.

So they entered Profitthorn the way careful rain enters stone.

Separately.

Quietly.

Hours apart.

Sometimes days.

One through commercial transit.

Another through freight certification work.

One under contract review cover.

Another as temporary systems consultant.

No two routes alike.

No cluster to observe.

No obvious shape.

Torlan approved.

Alexa called it paranoid.

With admiration.

The first to arrive was Lillian.

Though "arrive" hardly fit.

She simply appeared in the office one afternoon while Torlan was reviewing dispute filings.

He looked up.

She was already reading the board.

No greeting.

No announcement.

Only:

"This is ambitious."

Torlan blinked.

"You were expected tomorrow."

"I made good time."

Alexa looked amused.

"Do all your entrances ignore ordinary physics?"

"Only when necessary."

Lillian studied the words on the board.

Trap him.

Force decision.

Use control against him.

Then she said quietly:

"You may actually be serious."

Torlan answered,

"We feared you might notice."

She pointed to the board.

"This part interests me."

Which part?"

Make Kessler the mark."

She nodded.

"That may work."

Just like that.

No dramatic praise.

Only the dangerous approval of someone who understood structures.

That mattered deeply.

Two days later Marcus arrived.

Loudly, though unintentionally.

He entered the office reception carrying a travel case and looking around suspiciously.

"This city has too many polished surfaces."

Alexa looked up.

"You made it."

"Barely.

I was nearly killed by administrative signage."

He stopped in the conference room.

Looked at the expanded operation board.

Then at Torlan.

Then back at the board.

Slowly.

"You have gone mad."

Torlan considered.

"Possibly."

Marcus pointed.

"This says make Kessler the mark."

"Yes."

"That is not a sentence sane men write."

Lillian said without looking up,

"It's structurally elegant."

Marcus stared.

"Oh good.

Now there are two of you."

That helped.

More than anyone said.

Because suddenly the room felt inhabited again.

Not just strategic.

Alive.

Over the next several days others filtered in.

Never in ways inviting notice.

One used temporary audit credentials.

Another entered through contracted supply oversight.

One rented rooms across the district.

Another in a residential tower three levels away.

Separate lodgings.

Separate routines.

As planned.

The office, however—

slowly changed.

Unused side rooms gained occupants.

Empty desks acquired papers.

Quiet corridors acquired whispered debates.

The oversized conference room no longer felt oversized.

Alexa noticed first.

She stood in the doorway watching people work.

Then said softly:

"Well."

Torlan glanced up.

Again?"

"It appears your 'for now' was prophecy."

He looked around.

She was right.

The office had become something else.

Not a consultancy.

Not yet a conspiracy.

Something between.

A preparation.

A stage.

The word stage stayed with him.

That evening the full team gathered in the central conference room for the first time.

Doors secured.

Voices low.

Maps spread.

The board looming.

Marcus looked around.

"I assume one of you intends to explain why I crossed half a sector to join what appears to be a criminal brainstorming society."

Alexa said,

"We prefer strategic initiative."

"Of course you do."

Torlan stepped to the board.

And for the first time—

laid out the shape.

Kessler.

Fear system.

Garron.

Possible hidden ledgers.

A sting not yet fully formed.

No one interrupted.

Which was unusual.

And revealing.

When he finished—

silence.

"This is impossible."

Marcus paused.

Then said, "Continue."

That was essentially endorsement.

Lillian pointed to one section.

"If Kessler is to become mark…"

she tapped the board,

"he must be made to trust the false sequence."

Torlan looked at her.

Exactly.

Others began adding thoughts.

Complications.

Roles.

Questions.

The room came alive.

Not with agreement.

With intelligence.

Hours passed.

At one point Marcus leaned back and muttered,

"I miss simple missions."

No one believed him.

Near midnight discussion thinned.

Plans remained rough.

But one thing had changed.

The sting no longer belonged to two minds.

It had become shared architecture.

That mattered Immensely.

As the others drifted out in pairs and fragments, Marcus lingered.

Looked once at the board.

Then at Torlan.

Quietly:

"You believe this can work?"

Torlan considered.

Then:

"I believe it can fail brilliantly."

Marcus stared.

"That is not comforting."

"No."

Then after a pause:

"But yes.

I think it may work."

Marcus nodded once. It was good enough.

At the office door he stopped.

"One thought."

Torlan waited.

"If Kessler truly controls people through fear…"

"Yes?"

Marcus smiled faintly.

"Perhaps friendship may prove inconvenient."

That line stayed.

After everyone left, the office had gone quiet again.

But different quiet.

A Full, prepared quiet.

Torlan stood alone in the conference room.

Looked at occupied desks.

Closed side offices.

Maps.

Notes.

Friends.

A team gathered inside the machine.

And suddenly he realized—

the sting had already begun long before Kessler knew it.

Not when Kessler moved.

Now.

When the right people had quietly taken their places.

He looked once more at the board.

Then added a final note beneath all the others.

Build the stage.

He stepped back.

Read it.

And nodded.

Yes.

That was next.

And somewhere far above,

in his own polished offices,

Kessler went on believing every movement in Exchange Spire obeyed his design.

For now.

## Chapter 11 - Building the Stage

By the time the full team had been in place a week, the conference room no longer resembled a room where ordinary business could plausibly occur.

Too many maps.

Too many coded notes.

Too many dangerous ideas written in careful handwriting.

Marcus had begun referring to it as

"the room in which reasonable judgment comes to die."

Alexa considered that unfair.

Only slightly.

Tonight the full team sat around the broad conference table debating one stubborn question.

If Kessler was the mark—

where was the pressure point?

Torlan stood near the board.

"Kessler is too insulated."

Heads nodded.

"Then pressure reaches him indirectly."

Lillian leaned back.

"Through something he trusts."

"Or someone," Alexa said.

That hung in the room.

Someone.

Marcus frowned.

“We assume there is such a person?”

“There almost has to be,” Torlan said.

“No architect runs hidden structures alone.”

Silence.

Then Marcus muttered,

“Some poor soul keeps his sins alphabetized.”

Alexa looked up.

Oddly, that line stayed.

Later that afternoon, in a lower-level café during a break in arguments and overthinking, the first breadcrumb appeared.

By accident.

Or what passes for accident in good investigations.

Two clerks at a nearby table were talking too loudly for people discussing internal accounting.

One said:

“That Quill fellow gives me chills.”

The other laughed.

“If anyone knows where the bodies are buried, it’s Quill.”

The remark was tossed away casually.

But Torlan and Alexa both went still.

Marcus noticed first.

“What?”

Alexa said quietly,

“Did you hear that?”

Marcus blinked.

“The bodies buried part?”

Torlan was already listening again.

But the clerks had moved on to something unimportant.

Too late.

Yet enough.

Back in the office the name was on the board within minutes.

MARVEN QUILL

Circled.

Underlined.

Question mark beside it.

Lillian pulled personnel archives.

There he was.

Senior variance accountant.

Restricted reconciliation authority.

Unusual access permissions.

Deep internal routing privileges.

Alexa looked up slowly.

"Well."

Torlan almost smiled.

Useful word indeed.

Marcus leaned over the records.

"This man appears to have been born suspicious."

Lillian pointed to access logs.

"He enters sectors most senior executives do not."

Torlan studied the pattern.

Too much access for a mere accountant.

Far too much.

Alexa said,

"If anyone stands near hidden structures…"

She let it hang.

No need finishing.

Everyone saw it.

Quill might be the pressure point.

Or the path to it.

But rumor was not enough.

Torlan said so.

"We need confirmation."

Marcus folded his arms.

"How?"

Silence.

Then Lillian said quietly,

"We listen."

Everyone looked at her.

She tapped a service schematic.

Waste routing.

Maintenance conduits.

Apex Chamber perimeter.

Torlan's eyes narrowed.

Alexa smiled.

That was usually dangerous.

Marcus looked around slowly.

"I dislike the look all three of you have."

No one reassured him.

By midnight a micro recorder sat hidden in the automated waste chute near Kessler's executive sector.

A tiny act.

Potentially enormous consequences.

Then came waiting.

Always waiting.

Which Marcus claimed was the worst part of espionage and dentistry alike.

Three days later the recorder was recovered.

The whole team gathered in the conference room.

Lights low.

Doors secured.

No one joking now.

Alexa queued the recovered snippet.

Pressed play.

Static.

Soft hum.

Footsteps.

Then:

Kessler's voice.

Cold.

Measured.

Unmistakable.

"Quill sees everything."

A second voice:

"He's the only one who understands the deeper layers."

Then Kessler again:

"If something goes wrong, Quill will know before any of us."

Silence.

Recorder hiss.

End.

No one moved.

Marcus finally said,

"Well."

This time no one teased him.

Torlan replayed it.

Again.

And again.

Each time the words grew heavier.

Not speculation now.

Confirmation.

Lillian broke silence first.

"He's the nerve center."

Alexa nodded.

"Or close to it."

Marcus leaned back slowly.

"We were looking for a weak seam."

He pointed at the speaker.

"We just found a human one."

Exactly.

Torlan stood.

Walked to the board.

Beneath KESSLER he wrote:

QUILL

Then drew a line between them.

The room watched.

Quiet and focused.

Then Torlan said:

"We do not begin with Kessler."

No one spoke.

He turned.

"We begin with Quill."

The sentence changed everything.

The sting had found its first living target.

Marcus rubbed his jaw.

"So."

"We are planning to unsettle a secretive accountant who frightens his coworkers and apparently knows where hidden structures live."

Alexa looked up.

"Yes."

Marcus sighed.

"Good.
I merely wished to hear how unreasonable we've become."
Needed laughter followed.
Brief, welcome laughter followed.
Then strategy began changing.
Not theoretical now.
Practical.
If Quill mattered—
he must be studied.
Routine.
Habits.
Weaknesses.
Access.
Everything.
A surveillance board began growing almost immediately.
Coffee alcove?
Meal patterns?
Office hours?
Who speaks with him?
Who avoids him?
Lillian pointed to Quill's records.
"He takes coffee at nine every morning."
Marcus blinked.
"Even sinister accountants need rituals."
Alexa wrote:
9 A.M. COFFEE ALCOVE
Torlan noticed.
A small thing.
Yet perhaps not.
It was striking how stings often begin with tiny habits.

Not grand crimes.

Coffee.

Schedules.

Routine.

The ordinary.

Exactly where deception likes to hide.

Hours later, when most had drifted out, Marcus lingered.

Looking at Quill's name.

Then said quietly,

"Do you realize…"

Torlan waited.

"This may be the moment we stopped investigating corruption…"

He pointed at the board.

"…and began planning a sting."

Torlan looked at QUILL circled beneath Kessler.

Then nodded.

"Yes."

Marcus gave a faint smile.

"I was afraid of that."

After he left, Torlan remained alone.

Rear atrium lights glowing beyond glass.

The board before him.

Kessler.

Quill.

A line between.

A bridge—or perhaps a trap.

He added one final note beneath Quill's name.

Study the accountant.

Then below that:

Build the snare.

He stepped back.

Read it.

Felt something settle.

The next move was no longer abstract.

It had a face.

Marven Quill.

Somewhere in the upper machinery of Exchange Spire,

likely still balancing invisible crimes in perfect order—

utterly unaware

he had become the first piece moved in a game he did not know existed.

For now.

## Chapter 12 - The Accountant

Marven Quill did not disappoint expectations.

He exceeded them.

Unfortunately.

Three days into observing him, Marcus announced over breakfast in the conference room:

"I believe your accountant may be assembled from filing cabinets and regret."

Alexa looked up from notes.

"That is unkind."

"It is accurate."

Torlan said nothing.

Because Marcus was not entirely wrong.

Quill was a man of severe economy.

Economy of movement.

Economy of speech.

Possibly economy of soul.

He arrived at nearly the same hour each morning.

Never early.

Never late.

Dark suit.

Same narrow case.

Same measured stride.

He acknowledged no one unless required.

And even then, acknowledgment looked like administrative discomfort.

Marcus had taken to narrating Quill sightings in a tone usually reserved for wildlife documentaries.

"Observe the cautious ledger creature…"

Alexa forbade this twice.

It did not help.

Surveillance rotated quietly.

No patterns.

No tails obvious enough to matter.

The team observed.

Logged.

Waited.

And Quill—without knowing it—began teaching them how to approach him.

That was the key.

Not forcing weakness.

Studying routine until opportunity appeared.

Torlan liked that.

Because it felt less like invention.

More like discovery.

Quill's habits proved almost mechanical.

Lunch at 12:14.

Always alone.

Office return 12:42.

A walk through reconciliation corridors at 3:10.

And most interesting—

coffee at precisely nine.

Every day.

Same alcove.

Same table.

Same chair.

Marcus looked at the surveillance chart.

"He is either a genius accountant…"

"…or haunted clockwork."

Lillian said dryly,

"Possibly both."

The coffee alcove itself sat in a quiet administrative corridor far enough from heavy traffic to feel private but public enough to appear safe.

Perfectly Quill.

Alexa circled it on a floor plan.

"Routine is invitation."

Torlan nodded.

Maybe.

Possibly more.

They began taking turns observing from different angles.

Sometimes as consultants.

Sometimes as clerical staff.

Sometimes simply background.

Invisible.

Or nearly.

And slowly Quill became less abstraction.

More person.

Strange person.

But person.

He read printed financial bulletins while drinking coffee.

On paper.

Paper.

Marcus found this offensive.

"In a digital civilization."

Quill folded each section precisely.

Returned it neatly.

Never left crumbs.

Never glanced idly.

Never relaxed.

Alexa noticed something first.

"Watch his hands."

Torlan did.

Still.

Except when turning pages.

Then—

restless.

Interesting. A hidden strain worth noting.

Another day she said,

"He startles when approached."

Torlan watched.

She was right.

Not outwardly.

Microseconds.

Enough.

A cautious man.

Maybe fearful.

Maybe merely secretive.

Potentially useful distinction.

Then came the small moment that shifted observation.

A minor thing.

But not minor.

One morning Quill arrived at the coffee alcove carrying two folders.

A junior clerk brushed him accidentally.

One folder nearly slipped.

Quill reacted with startling force.

Snatched it back.

Sharp.

Almost panicked.

Then instantly composed himself.

But too late.

Torlan had seen it.

So had Alexa.

Marcus whispered,

"There."

Yes.

There.

A seam.

Fear around records.

That afternoon in conference room debate turned serious.

Marcus pointed at surveillance board.

"He guards information physically."

"Yes," Torlan said.

Alexa added,

"And startles under interruption."

Lillian:

"He dislikes unpredictability."

The room quieted.

Because now they were no longer merely describing Quill.

They were beginning to understand leverage.

A dangerous but useful moment.

Marcus leaned back.

"You are all thinking the same thing."

No one denied it.

He sighed.

"I was afraid of that."

Torlan stood.

Walked to board.

Under QUILL he wrote:

ORDER

ROUTINE

CONTROL

Then after a pause:

DISRUPTION

Circled it.

The room watched.

Alexa said softly,

"That may be how he opens."

Torlan nodded.

Perhaps.

The first whisper of snatch logic hovered there—

not yet formed.

But close.

That evening an unexpected development nearly broke the routine.

Quill did something unscheduled.

He left his office late.

Took an interior lift to restricted archival levels.

Stayed nearly two hours.

Returned carrying nothing.

Marcus stared at surveillance notes.

"Well."

Again the word.

But justified.

Lillian tapped the record.

"Archival annex."

Torlan looked up.

The phrase stirred.

Garron.

Books.

Vault.

Something connected.

Perhaps.

Not enough yet.

But suggestive.

The accountant was becoming doorway.

Which changed everything.

Later, over cold coffee and too many notes, Marcus said:

"Question."

Torlan waited.

"When exactly did we begin studying a man's beverage habits as prelude to abduction?"

Alexa answered without looking up.

"Probably Tuesday."

Marcus nodded.

Then after a pause:

"I'm not opposed.

I merely like chronology."

Needed laughter.

Again.

Then something unexpected happened.

Small.

Human.

Complicating.

During one observation shift, Alexa returned unusually quiet.

Torlan noticed.

“What?”

She hesitated.

Then:

“I almost felt sorry for him.”

That surprised even her.

Marcus looked scandalized.

“For the accountant?”

She shrugged.

“He looks lonely.”

Silence.

A thoughtful silence followed.

Torlan considered.

Important point.

Because monsters are easier to use than men.

Quill might be neither.

Exactly.

That mattered.

After a long pause Torlan said,

“Do not forget he may be trapped too.”

That stayed in room.

And perhaps—

though no one said it—

it planted the first seed that Quill might someday turn.

Near midnight the team gathered around the surveillance board one final time.

Patterns clear now.

Routine established.

Coffee alcove circled red.

Nine a.m.

Again and again.

Marcus read the board.

Then said:

"If someone wished to interrupt Mr. Clockwork's universe…"

he tapped the circled alcove,

"…one might begin there."

No one disagreed.

Torlan looked at the marked floor plan.

Then wrote beneath it:

THE OPENING

He stepped back.

Read it.

Yes.

That was right.

Not the snatch.

Not yet.

The opening.

Outside, Exchange Spire hummed in layered night silence.

Somewhere above,

Marven Quill was likely balancing hidden accounts beneath bright desk lamps—

utterly unaware that a roomful of patient strangers now knew the rhythm of his coffee.

And sometimes, Torlan thought,

history turns not on wars.

But on small routines—

a chair,

a paper,

a startled hand,
nine a.m. coffee.
And perhaps—
a very careful interruption.
The opening had been found.

## Chapter 13 - The Snatch Plan

For two days no one said the word aloud.

Though everyone was thinking it.

That itself said enough.

The surveillance board had grown dense with patterns.

Coffee alcove.

Archival visits.

Restricted routes.

Quill's routines mapped with almost embarrassing precision.

And in the center—

that circled phrase:

THE OPENING.

The conference room felt quieter now.

Not from lack of discussion.

From the kind of thinking that narrows.

Dangerous thinking.

Measured thinking.

Marcus finally broke the silence.

"We are all contemplating kidnapping an accountant."

No one corrected him.

He nodded.

"I felt clarification might help."

Alexa looked up.

"We are contemplating removing a pressure point from a criminal structure."

Marcus stared.

"That is the longest phrase for kidnapping I have ever heard."

Lillian, without looking up, said,

"It is not inaccurate."

Marcus sighed.

"Now there are two of you."

Torlan had been studying Quill's coffee routine.

At last he said,

"We may have only one chance to reach him."

Heads turned.

The room tightened.

Because once Torlan said it aloud—

the unsaid became plan.

Not theory.

Plan.

Alexa folded her arms.

"Then we ask first whether we should."

Alexa folded her arms.

"Then we ask first whether we should."

No one rushed past it.

For a while the room debated not mechanics—

morality.

Risk.

Alternatives.

Could Quill simply be approached?

Too dangerous.

Too loyal perhaps.

Could he be turned through persuasion alone?

Unlikely.

Could evidence be reached without him?

Possibly.

But blind.

Dangerously blind.

Every route bent back to Quill.

Marcus leaned back.

"So our least unreasonable option…"

He looked around.

"…is apparently the unreasonable one."

Torlan nodded once.

"Yes."

Silence.

Then the crossing happened.

Lillian spread a floor plan of the coffee alcove.

"Suppose," she said quietly,

"we stop debating whether…"

…and begin asking how."

There.

Threshold crossed.

The room knew it.

Torlan moved to board.

Wrote one word:

EXTRACTION

Marcus looked offended.

"You renamed kidnapping."

"Operationally."

"Of course."

Lillian began.

"Public snatch impossible."

Agreed.

Too visible.

Too crude.

Alexa tapped the floor plan.

"But interruption…"

She circled the alcove.

"…might be made to appear ordinary."

Torlan looked at her.

"What kind of interruption?"

She hesitated.

Then—

almost casually—

"What if someone simply speaks to him?"

The room looked up.

She continued.

"Quill is unsettled by unexpected contact."

Yes.

They had seen it.

She leaned over the plan.

"At coffee.

A stranger approaches.

Small question.

Small distraction."

Marcus frowned.

"You intend to abduct him through politeness?"

Alexa said,

"It has worked before."

No one knew if she was joking.

Perhaps she didn't either.

Then Lillian added softly,

"A mild sedative."

Silence.

Marcus blinked.

And there it was.

The plan took first breath.

Torlan said slowly,

"Coffee."

Alexa nodded.

"Dropped during distraction."

Marcus stared around the room.

"I should object more strongly."

"Probably," Alexa said.

He considered.

"I am thinking about it."

Needed laughter.

Thin.

But real.

Now details began moving.

How long before effect?

How quickly remove him?

Where move him?

How unseen?

Every question sharpened the impossible into process.

At one point Torlan stopped discussion.

"One principle."

Everyone looked up.

"No improvisation."

Important.

Very.

"If this happens…"

he tapped the board,

"…every step is rehearsed."

Agreement all around.

Essential.

Then Marcus said,

"You still have not explained how unconscious accountants leave crowded corridors unnoticed."

Excellent point.

Lillian looked almost pleased.

"We have."

She pulled a logistics sketch.

Service route.

Maintenance access.

And a cargo crate.

Marcus stared.

No one spoke.

Then:

"You plan to put Quill in a box."

Temporary containment."

"Of course you do."

Alexa looked far too innocent.

"The crate appears heavy."

Marcus rubbed his forehead.

"I liked us better as consultants."

But even he was smiling now.

Because beneath absurdity—

the plan was disturbingly plausible.

And that was unsettling.

They spent hours refining.

Two disguised maintenance men.

Large equipment crate.

Timed approach.

Removal route.

Return path.

Every piece examined.

Then challenged.

Then rebuilt.

Near midnight Torlan stepped back.

Something bothered him.

"What?"

Alexa asked.

He pointed at Quill's name.

"This only works…"

"…if Quill survives the first shock."

Meaning psychologically.

Not physically.

Important distinction.

Lillian nodded.

"He must be frightened."

Marcus looked troubled.

"That part I dislike."

So did Torlan.

But truth mattered.

Sometimes uncomfortably.

Alexa said quietly,

"We are not breaking him."

Torlan looked at her.

"We are opening him."

Much discussion followed over what came after snatch.

Isolation?

Questioning?

Pressure?

No final answers yet.

Only seeds.

The Long Night lay far ahead.

Still unseen.

For now only extraction mattered.

And whether it could be done.

Finally Marcus looked around the room.

Then said,

"I regret to report..."

"...this may work."

Highest praise he ever gave.

At end of session Torlan wrote beneath THE OPENING:

THE SNATCH

Then below it:

REHEARSE EVERYTHING

He stepped back.

Read it.

No one joked.

Because now the sting had crossed another line.

It had entered mechanics.

As people began drifting out, Alexa lingered.

Studying the coffee alcove diagram.

Then quietly:

"You know what unsettles me?"

Torlan waited.

"That something so large..."

she tapped the page,

"...may turn on whether one distracted man reaches for coffee."

Torlan considered.

Then:

"Large systems often fail at small hinges."

She nodded.

Understood.

After she left, Torlan remained alone again.

That had become habit.

He looked at Quill's name.

At crate route sketches.

At dangerous ideas now wearing procedure.

And thought:

The stage is almost built.

Somewhere above,

Marven Quill would arrive tomorrow at nine.

Read his paper.

Drink his coffee.

Keep hidden books.

Preserve invisible crimes.

Entirely unaware

that strangers had just spent six hours deciding how to steal him from routine.

And in some quiet moral corner of himself—

Torlan recognized the truth.

There would be no returning to simple investigation now.

The sting had moved.

And next—

it would rehearse.

## Chapter 14 - Building the Stage

The plan became stranger once it began improving.

Marcus pointed this out twice.

No one denied it.

The snatch itself now seemed almost straightforward compared to what followed.

Because removing Quill was only the first deception.

Turning him—

that required theater.

And theater required a stage.

The phrase Torlan had written half-seriously on the board days earlier—

Build the stage—

had become operational instruction.

Quite literally.

The oversized office suite, once rented simply as cover, began changing.

Quietly.

Carefully.

Room by room.

The back corner storage office became the first transformation.

A holding cell.

Or rather—

what a frightened accountant should believe was one.

Temporary steel partition.

Narrow cot.

Security light.

Visible lock mechanism.

A surveillance lens mounted where Quill would notice it.

Marcus stood in doorway watching construction.

Then said:

"I should like history to remember I objected to counterfeit imprisonment."

Alexa looked up.

"You have objected continuously."

"I wish the record clear."

Lillian adjusted the false lock plate.

"It only needs to look convincing."

Marcus considered.

"That is somehow worse."

But he stayed and helped.

The central conference room changed next.

Table replaced.

Lighting altered.

Overhead lamp lowered harshly.

Neutral walls made colder.

A recorder placed visibly.

Two metal chairs.

Nothing dramatic.

Just official enough.

Unpleasant enough.

Believable enough.

Alexa stepped inside when it was done.

Stopped.

Looked around.

Then quietly:

"I dislike this room."

Torlan nodded.

"Good."

That was the point.

The illusion had to unsettle even them.

Otherwise it would not hold.

Marcus studied the room.

"This resembles every interrogation scene I've ever hoped not to enter."

Lillian said,

"Encouraging."

He looked offended.

Meanwhile wardrobe had become unexpectedly important.

A discovery Marcus found deeply suspicious.

Two members of team assembled what passed for detective attire.

Dark investigative suits.

Plain official coats.

Badges fabricated just credible enough to survive fear.

Even shoes mattered.

Apparently.

Marcus objected to his assigned jacket.

"It makes me look bureaucratic."

Alexa said,

"You are portraying law enforcement."

"Cruel."

Torlan ignored this.

Because details mattered.

Fear notices details.

And Quill—

they all suspected—

would notice everything.

Rehearsals began.

Not casually.

Meticulously.

Route from coffee alcove.

Crate timing.

Blindfold transfer.

The path through office corridors.

Even the deception of movement.

This fascinated Marcus.

"You mean," he said,

"after abducting him…"

He paused.

"…we walk him in circles?"

"Blindfolded."

"To make the office feel distant."

"Yes."

Marcus stared.

"This is either genius or sin."

No one resolved which.

But the blindfold route was practiced.

Again.

From rear holding room,
through connecting corridor,
around side offices,
into conference room.

So Quill would believe he had been taken elsewhere.

Brilliantly simple.

Torlan liked it immediately.

Because deception rooted in geography was elegant.

One afternoon they ran full rehearsal.

Everything.

From coffee approach to first interrogation.

Alexa played Quill.

A role she approached with unnerving seriousness.

Marcus objected.

"Your imitation of frightened accountants is disturbing."

"I researched."

Of course she had.

During rehearsal Lillian stopped the process twice over tiny inconsistencies.

Badge angle wrong.

Door sound wrong.

Timing too slow.

Marcus muttered,

"We are being defeated by realism."

Torlan quietly thought the illusion was sharpening.

Then came discussion of identity.

Who questions Quill first?

Who stays unseen?

Who plays sympathetic contrast?

That mattered deeply.

Because interrogation is often theater of roles.

Marcus volunteered reluctantly.

"I apparently radiate institutional disappointment."

Alexa would be first face Quill saw.

Unexpectedly gentle.

Unexpectedly unsettling.

Also useful.

Torlan would remain mostly unseen at first.

Presence withheld.

Authority implied.

The room approved.

Interesting how quickly absurd things become logical under pressure.

Late one night, after another rehearsal, Marcus stood in the mock holding room.

Hands in pockets.

Studying false cell bars.

Then said quietly:

"You know what troubles me?"

Torlan looked up.

"We are getting good at this."

That landed.

Because true.

And slightly alarming.

A necessary silence followed.

Then Alexa said,

"We should remain uncomfortable."

Torlan nodded.

"Yes."

Because discomfort meant conscience still lived.

One further problem remained.

What if Quill resisted physically?

Discussion grew serious there.

Restraints?

Minimal.

Only if required.

No roughness.

No harm.

Repeated principle.

This was pressure.

Not cruelty.

Finally Lillian raised something unexpected.

"If Quill wakes early in transit?"

Silence.

Then contingency planning.

Of course.

Alternate sedation timing.

Secondary response.

Backup route.

No gap left untested.

By now the operation had become almost embarrassingly thorough.

Marcus looked at the layered planning sheets.

"This may be the most effort anyone has devoted to confusing one accountant."

Near midnight Torlan walked alone through transformed rooms.

Reception.

Side offices.

Holding cell.

Interrogation room.

The false world they had built inside ordinary leased offices.

Remarkable and unsettling.

He stood in doorway of mock cell.

Imagined Quill waking there.

Believing everything lost.

The moral weight returned.

Heavy, but necessary.

Alexa appeared beside him.

Quietly.

"You're wondering if we've gone too far."

Not question.

Observation.

"Yes."

She nodded.

"So am I."

That helped.

More than reassurance would have.

Then she looked around the staged rooms.

And said softly:

"The strange thing…"

Torlan waited.

"…is it may work."

Yes—that was the unsettling part.

It might.

Before leaving, Torlan returned to the board.

Beneath THE SNATCH he wrote:

BUILD THE ILLUSION

Then beneath that:

MAKE HIM BELIEVE

He stared at it.

Read it twice.

And knew.

The next move would no longer be rehearsal.

It would be execution.

Somewhere above,
Marven Quill would sleep in perfect routine.

Unaware a false jail now waited.

A counterfeit interrogation room.

Fabricated detectives.

An office transformed into a theater of pressure.

And perhaps, Torlan thought, all great stings are part mathematics…

and part stagecraft.

The stage was ready.

Now only the actor remained.

## Chapter 15 - The Snatch

At 8:42 the conference room was silent.

Not ordinary silence.

Operational silence.

The kind made of concentration and checked watches.

Coffee sat untouched.

No one joked.

Even Marcus had gone solemn.

Which the others privately considered a notable atmospheric shift.

The plan had been rehearsed twelve times.

Every route timed.

Every gesture tested.

Every contingency argued.

Now rehearsal was gone.

Only execution remained.

Torlan stood at the board one last time.

The opening.

The snatch.

Build the illusion.

Make him believe.

All roads had narrowed to one small alcove.

One cup of coffee.

One distracted accountant.

History occasionally turned on stranger hinges.

Alexa adjusted the plain jacket she wore for first contact.

Marcus checked the maintenance disguise with theatrical disgust.

"I look like a man who repairs ventilation morally."

"No one has ever described you so accurately," Alexa said.

Brief, thin laughter came and went quickly.

Torlan looked at both.

"One last time."

The room stilled.

"No improvisation."

Heads nodded.

"No harm."

Again.

"If anything feels wrong…"

He let it hang.

Abort.

Understood without saying.

At 8:56 positions were taken.

Quietly.

Naturally.

As if routine.

Exactly as planned.

The coffee alcove sat in its usual muted stillness.

Paper stacked.

Morning traffic had not started yet.

Administrative corridors still carried the hush before the day fully gathered.

Which was precisely why the time had been chosen.

At 8:59 Marven Quill arrived.

Precisely.

Of course.

Dark suit.

Narrow case.

Morning bulletin folded under one arm.

Same chair.

Same table.

Same cup.

Same world.

Unaware.

At 9:00, two maintenance cleaners rolled quietly into the corridor, each carrying mops and service buckets.

Without haste they set yellow caution cones near the alcove access.

**Temporary floor treatment. Use adjacent corridor.**

Routine enough no one looked twice.

Casual enough to redirect foot traffic for several precious minutes.

The coffee alcove grew unexpectedly empty.

Which was the point.

Alexa watched from corridor turn.

Marcus from maintenance route.

Two disguised "workers" nearby with a large equipment crate whose weight appeared convincingly inconvenient.

All absurd.

All somehow plausible.

At 9:01 Alexa moved.

No hesitation.

She crossed to Quill's table carrying a newspaper.

Stopped.

"Excuse me," she said softly.

Quill looked up—

startled exactly as predicted.

A small thing, but a big seam.

She held up the paper.

"Is this today's financial edition?"

Quill blinked.

Unexpected contact clearly unsettling.

"Yes… I believe…"

He reached awkwardly toward his folded copy.

Fumbling slightly.

Trying to be helpful.

Trying to restore order.

In that tiny confusion—

a small tablet dropped soundlessly into his coffee.

Gone.

Invisible.

Routine broken.

Seed planted.

Alexa smiled.

"May I borrow the market section?"

Quill, visibly disoriented by mere social interaction, extracted pages with absurd earnestness.

Marcus would later call it
"the most polite abduction in criminal history."

At that moment, no one breathed.

Alexa thanked him.

Left.

Quill resumed coffee.

Paper.

Routine.

Almost.

At 9:05 his hand slowed turning a page.

At 9:06 he blinked hard.

At 9:07 he lowered head briefly.

At 9:08—

he slipped forward onto folded arms.

As though exhausted.

Sleeping accountant.

Nothing dramatic.

The two maintenance men moved at once.

Practiced.

Unhurried.

One muttered loudly enough for passersby:

"Poor fellow overdid it again."

Mild office sympathy.

No alarm.

They lifted Quill smoothly.

Into the open crate.

Lid closed.

Secured.

Gone.

By 9:10 the alcove was ordinary again.

Only an abandoned coffee cup remained.

History often leaves smaller footprints than expected.

The crate moved through service corridor.

Timed route.

Blind turns.

Maintenance access.

No interruption.

Torlan waited at office service entry.

When crate arrived—

only one word:

"Inside."

Door shut.

Operation phase one complete.

No celebration.

Only movement.

Blindfold applied.

Quill, still under light sedation, transferred to holding room cot.

False cell door locked.

Security light on.

Everything ready.

Then came waiting again.

At noon Quill stirred.

Slowly.

Confused.

Disoriented.

He opened his eyes to bars.

Cold light.

Unknown room.

His breathing changed at once.

Fear enters chest before face.

Torlan noticed.

Door opened.

Marcus entered first.

Now in detective coat.

Carrying a file.

Expression all bureaucratic disappointment.

Remarkably natural.

He looked at Quill as if late paperwork had inconvenienced him personally.

Quill tried to sit up.

"What is—"

Marcus cut him off.

Save it."

Then glanced at file.

"Marven Quill.

Senior reconciliation authority."

Cold.

Official.

Alexa entered behind him.

Set recorder on table outside cell.

Visible.

Intentional.

Quill stared.

Disbelief fighting panic.

Good.

Marcus said flatly:

"You were picked up yesterday."

Quill blinked.

Yesterday?

He frowned.

Memory fractured.

Exactly as hoped.

Marcus continued:

"You passed out during transfer."

A beat.

"Lucky for you."

"You're one of several senior staff brought in."

Quill froze.

Several.

Yes.

Let that work.

Marcus turned pages theatrically.

"We've already questioned others."

He let that settle.

"We have most answers."

He paused.

"So there is very little point lying to us now."

Quill swallowed.

Hard.

"What is this about?"

Marcus looked almost bored.

If you don't know…"

he closed file,

"…that is deeply unhelpful."

Alexa leaned in slightly.

Unexpectedly softer.

"We'll talk soon."

Then they left.

Just like that.

No interrogation.

Only dread.

Door shut.

Lock sound deliberate.

Quill alone.

To think.

To imagine.

To fear.

Exactly right.

As they walked back into conference room Marcus whispered:

"Well."

Torlan looked at him.

He grinned faintly.

"I believe…"

He paused,

"…we have stolen an accountant."

Even Torlan nearly laughed.

Nearly.

But not quite.

Because he knew—

the snatch had succeeded.

Now came the harder part.

Turning him.

He looked through observation lens into false cell.

Quill sat motionless on cot.

Trying to understand a world that had vanished between coffee and waking.

The illusion held.

The stage worked.

And somewhere above in Exchange Spire—

Kessler likely still believed Quill sat over ledgers this very hour.

Routine intact.

Control preserved.

For now.

Torlan looked through the glass once more.

Then quietly said:

"The long night begins."

And it did.

## Chapter 16 - First Questioning

Quill did not ask to leave.

Torlan noticed that first.

Most innocent men demand explanation.

Most guilty men demand counsel.

Quill—

simply tried to understand.

That told Torlan much.

Fear had already begun doing its work.

Hours passed slowly.

Deliberately.

The false holding cell remained lit.

Meals arrived irregularly.

No clocks visible.

No markers of time.

A small cruelty—

though necessary.

Disorientation rarely enters dramatically.

It accumulates.

By evening Quill had asked twice where he was.

No one answered.

By design.

When the cell door opened again he visibly startled.

The illusion still held.

Marcus stood outside bars.

File in hand.

Expression grave enough to discourage hope.

"Mr. Quill."

No response.

Then:

"It is your turn."

That phrase landed.

Your turn.

Meaning others.

Meaning sequence.

Meaning inevitability.

Exactly right.

Quill stood slowly.

Hands unsteady.

Blindfold again.

Walked the practiced circular route through office corridors while believing distance expanded.

A simple deception, practiced to seem convincing.

Marcus almost admired it.

Almost.

They seated Quill in the interrogation room.

Overhead lamp harsh.

Recorder visible.

Two chairs.

Cold table.

Everything as rehearsed.

Blindfold removed.

Quill blinked hard against light.

Looked around.

Fear sharpened.

Alexa sat across from him.
Unexpected.
Not what he expected from authority.
Useful.
Marcus remained standing behind.
Presence.
Pressure.
For several moments—
silence.
Deliberate.
Then Alexa opened a folder.
Most pages blank.
Quill need never know.
She looked up.
"We've spoken with the others."
There it was again.
The lie deepening.
Quill swallowed.
"What others?"
Marcus answered flatly:
"Do not insult us."
A flinch.
Small.
Real.
Good.
Alexa leaned forward.
"Mr. Quill—
you were not picked up because of bookkeeping irregularities."
"Those are minor."
Quill looked confused.

Even alarmed.

She continued quietly:

"This concerns conspiracy."

A much heavier word.

Intentionally.

Quill's breathing changed.

Marcus opened file.

"We already know about settlement diversions."

Another bluff.

Delivered as fact.

"We know about concealed reconciliation structures."

Quill stared.

Too long.

Marcus saw recognition.

Not guilt proven.

But pressure found.

He said coldly:

"You react as if terms are familiar."

Quill spoke too quickly.

"I don't know what—"

Marcus slammed file shut.

Sharp sound.

Quill jumped.

Marcus leaned in.

"We told you lying wastes time."

Then sat.

Suddenly calmer.

More dangerous.

Alexa softened.

Unexpected contrast.

"Mr. Quill…

others have already been helpful."

That word—

helpful—

Sounds merciful.

Feels terrifying.

She lowered voice.

"You may help yourself too."

Quill said nothing.

Only stared at table.

Thinking.

Calculating.

Fear moving.

Torlan watched through hidden observation lens.

This was working.

Not breaking.

Opening.

Exactly as hoped.

Marcus changed direction abruptly.

"Why does Kessler trust you?"

Quill blinked.

Unexpected question.

Destabilizing.

"What?"

Marcus repeated.

"Why you?"

Silence.

Long.

Then Quill said quietly,

"I keep records."

Marcus:

"All records?"

Another pause.

Too long again.

Alexa noticed his hands.

Fingers tightening.

Exactly like coffee observations.

Same stress tell.

Consistency mattered.

She asked gently,

"Mr. Quill…

what are the deeper layers?"

The room froze.

Because that phrase.

From the recording.

Weaponized now.

Quill looked up sharply.

Too sharp.

He knew it.

And knew they knew something.

Marcus saw it too.

His voice went cold.

"How do we know that phrase?"

No answer.

Perfect.

Quill had just been trapped by surprise.

And knew it.

He tried recovery.

Failed.

"I want representation."

Marcus looked almost bored.

"You are in no position for procedural requests."

Cruel, but believable—and necessary.

Then Marcus stood.

Gathered file.

As if done.

Most unsettling move of all.

Ending before confession.

Quill panicked slightly.

Wait—"

Tiny word.

Huge crack.

Alexa noticed.

So did Torlan.

There.

The first pull toward cooperation.

Marcus turned slowly.

"Yes?"

Quill hesitated.

Said nothing.

Too frightened.

Too early.

Marcus gave almost disappointed nod.

"We'll continue tonight."

Night.

Let that word work.

Then he added:

"Perhaps after we compare your answers against the others."

Another twist of knife.

Door opened.

Closed.

Lock sound deliberate.

Quill alone again.

The silence afterward heavier than questioning.

As intended.

Back in conference room Marcus exhaled.

"Well."

Alexa smiled faintly.

"That went better than kidnapping usually does."

Marcus looked offended.

"How many are you comparing?"

Needed laugh.

Short.

But real.

Then serious again.

Torlan entered from observation room.

No one spoke for moment.

Then he said:

"He's beginning to imagine a case against him."

That was objective.

Not confession.

Self-generated dread.

Much stronger.

Alexa nodded.

"The deeper layers question shook him."

Marcus leaned against table.

"He is afraid we know more than we do."

Torlan:

"Good.

Soon he may convince himself we know everything."

That was where pressure ripens.

The long night approaching.

Before returning Quill to cell, Alexa passed him once in corridor.

Stopped.

Quietly.

Almost compassionate.

She said:

"If I were you…"

Quill looked up.

"…I'd start deciding who reaches truth first.

You—

or Kessler."

Then she walked away.

In the cell Quill sat long after lights dimmed.

Not sleeping.

Thinking.

Exactly as hoped.

And somewhere in those thoughts—

perhaps for first time—

Kessler may have appeared not protector.

But threat.

Only a seed. But enough.

Torlan watched through observation lens.

Then quietly said:

"Tonight we let fear work alone."

Marcus looked over.

"And tomorrow?"

Torlan answered:

"Tomorrow…

we let doubt help."

And the long night moved closer.

## Chapter 17 - The Long Night

Night was chosen for a reason.

Fear enlarges after dark.

Marcus claimed this was universal law.

No one argued.

After the first questioning Quill was returned to the false cell in silence.

No further threats.

No raised voices.

No dramatic pressure.

Which unsettled him more.

Pressure withdrawn can be more frightening than pressure applied.

Torlan counted on that.

Hours passed.

The office outside dimmed.

Voices lowered.

Footsteps grew infrequent.

The staged world seemed to settle into institutional night.

Exactly as intended.

Quill sat on the cot unmoving for long stretches.

Thinking.

Replaying.

Trying to assemble reality from fragments.

Dangerous work. Useful, too.

Near midnight Alexa entered alone.

Not as interrogator.

Almost as observer.

She carried a metal cup.

Set it down.

Water.

A gesture almost kind.

Deliberately so.

Quill looked up.

Exhausted already.

She said quietly:

"You should sleep."

He gave a hollow laugh.

"I don't think that is possible."

She studied him.

Then said softly—

as though perhaps she should not:

"They spoke with Kessler today."

Quill froze.

She let silence work.

Then:

"He was… cooperative."

And left.

Door shut.

No explanation.

Only poison.

Quill did not touch the water for a long time.

An hour later Marcus entered.

Different energy.

Administrative.

Cold.

File in hand.

He opened the bars.

"Come."

No explanation.

Blindfold again.

Circular route again.

Though this time Quill's uncertainty made distance feel endless.

By design.

In interrogation room lights seemed harsher.

Quill seated.

File placed before him.

Marcus remained standing.

Alexa absent.

Important.

Isolation.

Marcus opened folder.

Produced a signed statement.

Heavy paper.

Official formatting.

Visible signature.

Kessler's.

Or what appeared so.

Marcus slid it across.

"We appreciate Mr. Kessler's cooperation."

Quill stared.

Breathing altered instantly.

Marcus continued flatly:

"His testimony has been useful."

"As things stand…"

he tapped document,

"…he may be released today."

Then the knife:

"You, however, now appear primary."

Quill looked physically struck.

He read.

Hands trembling.

Statement claimed:

Marven Quill maintained unauthorized shadow ledgers.

Marven Quill initiated concealed transfer schemes.

Marven Quill acted independently.

Kessler had allegedly "reported irregular suspicions."

Beautifully treacherous.

Quill whispered:

No."

Marcus:

"It is signed."

Quill looked up.

"He wouldn't—"

Marcus leaned in.

"He already did."

That landed like death.

The room went silent.

Even Marcus almost pitied him.

Almost.

Quill looked smaller now.

Not physically.

Internally.

Then Marcus gathered the paper.

Conversation over.

No demand.

No offer.

Just betrayal.

Quill was returned to cell.

Shaking.

And sometime later—

the second phase began.

Light sedative in evening water.

Just enough.

Not heavy.

Dream-thin.

And as Quill drifted in uneasy half-sleep—

voices began.

Not from people.

From hidden speakers.

Soft.

Distant.

Almost dream.

A radio drama of accusation.

Blurred.

Surreal.

Kessler's voice.

Cold.

"We let Quill carry everything."

Another voice.

Police tone.

"He admits enough already."

Another.

"The accountant takes the fall."

Then Kessler again—

most brutal of all:

"He was always expendable."

Fragments.

Repeating.

Overlapping.

Not coherent enough to seem staged.

Perfectly dreamlike.

Quill stirred in sleep.

Sweat.

Half waking.

Unsure what was dream.

What was memory.

What was prophecy.

Torlan watched from darkened observation room.

Said almost nothing.

No need.

The machinery was working.

Near dawn Quill woke suddenly.

Disoriented.

Light harsh.

Silence absolute.

For several moments he looked unsure whether night had happened.

Or been nightmare.

Then—

through bars—

a paper lay on floor.

The signed statement.

Again.

Left there.

As if forgotten.

He stared at it.

Read Kessler's name.

Again.

And something changed.

Not broken.

Shifted.

Trust ruptured.

Far deeper.

Later, just before dawn, Alexa entered.

Looked at him.

Long silence.

Then:

"You had a difficult night."

Quill whispered,

"He betrayed me."

Not question.

Realization.

The line they needed.

Alexa said softly,

"We wondered when you'd see that."

She left.

Door shut.

Quill sat motionless.

Then head in hands.

The first collapse not into confession—

but into loneliness.

Which often comes first.

Always.

Back in conference room Marcus looked at Torlan.

"Well."

No humor now.

Only gravity.

Torlan said quietly:

"He will talk."

Marcus nodded.

"Yes."

Marcus paused. "Tomorrow."

And both knew.

Tomorrow Quill would not be resisting the investigators.

He would be trying to survive Kessler.

Entirely different posture.

As dawn reached the atrium windows,

Exchange Spire above began another perfect morning.

Employees arriving.

Systems moving.

Ledgers balancing.

Kessler perhaps already at work.

Unaware that in a false cell below,

the one man who kept his hidden books had just spent a night learning he was disposable.

And sometimes—

Torlan thought—

a man does not break because truth corners him.

He breakswhen loyalty dies.

Morning was coming.

And with it—

Quill's turn.

## Chapter 18 - Quill Breaks

By morning Quill looked older.

One night had done that.

Torlan had seen it before.

Not age.

Disillusion.

A harsher erosion.

The man brought into the interrogation room at dawn was not the same man taken from the coffee alcove.

Something internal had shifted.

Important things had shifted.

He sat before being told.

Another change.

Submission often arrives in tiny gestures first.

Alexa noticed.

So did Marcus.

No blindfold this time.

Deliberate.

Small sign things had advanced.

The overhead lamp glowed.

Recorder visible.

The false case file lay open.

And the signed statement—

placed where Quill could see it.

No one mentioned it.

No need.

It already spoke.

For a long while no one questioned him.

Silence again.

But now different.

Invitation.

Not threat.

Quill stared at the table.

Then quietly said,

"He would have done it."

Marcus did not pretend confusion.

"Kessler?"

A nod.

Barely.

"He would have let me carry everything."

First admission.

Not about crimes.

About betrayal.

Necessary first.

Alexa leaned forward.

"When did you realize that?"

Long pause.

Then:

"When I saw the statement."

His voice almost hollow.

Marcus said nothing.

Let him keep walking.

Quill surprised them.

He continued without prompting.

"I thought…"

he stopped.

Started again.

"I thought we were aligned."

There.

That word.

Aligned.

Very Quill.

Very revealing.

Alexa asked softly,

"You believed you were partners."

He gave faint bitter laugh.

"Yes."

Not denial.

Recognition.

Important.

Marcus opened the file.

Then quietly:

"Mr. Quill—

did you participate?"

At last.

The true question.

Long silence.

Then—

"Yes."

Simple.

No defense.

Good.

Torlan watching behind lens felt something settle.

The break had begun.

Marcus asked:

"How deeply?"

Quill looked up.

Tired eyes.

"All of it."

The room held still.

Then Quill said something no one expected.

"I improved some of it."

Alexa blinked.

Quill continued, words coming faster now.

"The diversions.

Layered transfers.

Shadow balancing.

Some were mine."

He almost seemed confessing to himself.

Not them.

Marcus asked,

"You suggested improvements."

"Yes."

A whisper.

"I made them harder to trace."

Alexa asked carefully,

"Why?"

Quill gave strange expression.

As if answer obvious.

"Because they worked."

Honest.

Cold.

Then after a pause:

"And because Kessler admired efficiency."

It explained everything.

Quill had served not merely greed—
but approval.
A deep and tragically human motive.
Marcus asked quietly,
"And you thought loyalty protected you."
Quill looked almost ashamed.
"Yes."
Then:
"I was a fool."
No one contradicted him.
Not needed.
Silence did more.
Then Marcus placed hand lightly on false confession statement.
"And now?"
Quill stared at Kessler's signature.
Then said words they had been waiting for:
"I want responsibility where it belongs."
Torlan exhaled slowly.
There it was.
Marcus leaned forward.
"Then help us."
No theatrics.
No triumph.
Just invitation.
Quill looked up.
Very long pause.
Then nodded.
Once.
Enough.
Alexa opened blank legal pad.

"Start with hidden ledgers."

And Quill began.

At first haltingly.

Then with gathering precision.

Because numbers were native tongue.

Locations.

False ownership chains.

Payoff schedules.

Weekly covert distributions.

Names.

Shell structures.

And then—

the vault.

He stopped there.

The room changed.

Marcus looked up.

"The vault?"

Quill nodded.

Voice almost mechanical now.

"Archival annex."

Torlan, behind observation glass, went still.

There.

The hidden chamber.

Real.

Quill continued:

"Manual ledgers."

Plural.

"Two primary books."

He hesitated.

Then:

"There is a third."

Marcus and Alexa exchanged glance.

The Third Ledger.

The old breadcrumb now flowering.

Quill saw it.

"You knew there were three?"

Marcus answered simply:

"We suspected."

Let him believe more.

Always.

Quill leaned back.

Spent.

Then something unexpectedly raw surfaced.

"I did terrible things."

The room quieted.

Alexa asked softly,

"Do you regret them?"

Long silence.

Then:

"I regret believing intelligence excused corruption."

That may be the truest line Quill speaks.

Marcus almost looked moved.

Almost.

Then Quill added:

"I thought Kessler and I would stand together."

"We built some of it together."

"I never imagined he'd offer me to save himself."

There lay the wound.

Still bleeding.

Driving confession.

Perfect.

At length Marcus said,

"We'll need access details."

Quill nodded.

"Yes."

And with that—

they moved from confession…

to operation.

Hours later, after pages of notes, Quill looked emptied.

But lighter.

Strange paradox.

Truth sometimes does that.

Before being returned to cell, he stopped at door.

Turned.

And quietly said:

"If Kessler knows I spoke…"

He did not finish.

No need.

Marcus answered:

"Then we move before he learns."

And there the next act began.

Vault.

Ledgers.

Endgame.

After Quill was taken back, Marcus entered observation room.

Looked at Torlan.

"Well."

Torlan almost smiled.

"He broke."

Marcus shook head.

"No."

He looked through glass at Quill.

"He woke."

Torlan nodded.

Yes.

Woke.

And somewhere high in Exchange Spire,

Kessler continued his perfect morning—

unaware the accountant who helped build his hidden crimes

had just begun dismantling them.

Piece by piece.

From the inside.

## Chapter 19 - The Hidden Vault

Quill did not offer the vault all at once.

He surrendered it reluctantly.

As though speaking of it aloud made betrayal real.

Torlan understood.

Some secrets resist even confession.

The interrogation room table was cleared except for a single building schematic Quill had drawn from memory.

No digital maps.

No network overlays.

Hand drawn.

Appropriately.

Because the vault itself distrusted systems.

Marcus stared at the sketch.

"This is hidden inside a records annex?"

Quill nodded.

"Behind preservation archives."

Alexa frowned.

"No guards?"

"None."

That surprised everyone.

Quill almost seemed offended.

"Guards attract notice."

He tapped the sketch.

"The vault protects itself."

Torlan leaned in.

"Explain."

And Quill did.

The access door was not visible as a door.

Only a recessed archival wall section behind rolling records stacks.

Unmarked.

No signage.

No code panel obvious from outside.

Because anyone seeing a vault entrance had already been told too much.

Very Kessler.

Marcus muttered,

"I dislike invisible doors."

No one disagreed.

Quill pointed.

"Mechanical latch behind third shelf support."

Manual release.

Old world.

No electronics exposed.

Torlan liked this immediately.

Machines can be hacked.

Paranoia often prefers metal.

Quill continued.

"Inside entry chamber there is timing."

He looked at each of them.

"Every step matters."

The room quieted.

Because Quill's tone had changed.

Now they were hearing priestly instruction.

Not accounting.

He held up a finger.

"Step one."

Door opens.

Enter.

Close it fully.

"Wait seven seconds."

Marcus blinked.

"Seven?"

"Yes."

"Why?"

Pressure equalization."

Silence.

Marcus looked around.

"I repeat.

I dislike invisible doors."

Quill ignored him.

"Move sooner…"

he tapped table,

"…silent alarm."

Move later…"

another tap,

"…secondary lock."

No one wrote slowly anymore.

Pens flew.

This mattered deeply.

Step two.

Three floor tiles in.

Pause.

Do not step on fourth black seam.

Pressure trigger.

Marcus said,

"There is a floor that objects to feet."

"Yes."

"Wonderful."

Quill almost did not smile.

Almost.

Then came ledger chamber.

Small.

Climate controlled.

Three pedestal shelves.

Two visible ledgers.

One concealed.

The Third Ledger.

Stored behind false back panel.

Marcus whispered,

Of course there is."

Of course.

Quill looked at Torlan.

"You remove only specified books."

"Why?"

Weight."

Quill explained.

Each book's pedestal calibrated.

Weight-sensitive.

Remove a ledger without replacement—

alarm.

Torlan looked slowly up.

"So replacement must match."

Quill nodded.

Exactly.

Lillian set two blank ledgers on table.

The ones prepared days earlier.

At last their purpose revealed.

Quill instructed:

"Weigh originals.

Match with blank replacements."

Pages removed from blanks until weight identical.

Marcus stared.

"We are counterfeiting gravity."

Alexa:

"Operationally."

Marcus closed eyes briefly.

No help for him.

The room now moved like engineers.

Questions rapid.

No wasted words.

What about exit?

Ah, most important.

Quill tapped diagram.

"Leaving is harder."

Of course.

Because theft often hides in exits.

The door reseals on manual sequence.

Leave wrong—

timestamp anomaly appears in my office."

Marcus looked up.

"Meaning Kessler could see entry?"

Quill nodded.

"If not erased."

Torlan:

"Can it be erased?"

Quill:

Yes."

He pause.

"If done before routine sync."

"How long?"

"Four minutes."

Silence.

Now the room tightened.

Four minutes.

That changes everything.

This was no burglary.

It was choreography.

Torlan asked quietly,

"Can you guide us through it?"

Quill looked at him.

Long.

Then:

"Yes."

Simple word.

Heavy.

They spent six hours rehearsing verbally.

Again.

Again.

Again.

Quill making them repeat sequence until he was satisfied.

Seven seconds.

Third tile.

Skip black seam.

Replace weight.

False back panel.

Reseal.

Erase timestamp.

Exit.

repeated the sequence again and again.

Marcus finally groaned:

"If I die in an archival vault…"

he looked upward,

"…I shall be offended eternally."

Needed laughter.

Thin.

But necessary.

Then Quill grew unexpectedly severe.

"If you improvise…"

he looked at all of them,

"…you fail."

Torlan nodded.

No improvisation.

Old principle.

Still true.

Near midnight Quill stopped them.

"There is one more thing."

Everyone looked up.

He hesitated.

Interesting.

Then:

"Kessler visits perhaps twice yearly."

Pause.

"I visit twice a week."

That mattered enormously.

Because only Quill belongs there.

No one else.

Which means any anomaly screams.

High stakes raised.

Marcus said softly,

"This is not entering a vault."

No."

Torlan answered.

"It is impersonating Quill."

Before ending session Quill took the blank ledgers.

Adjusted page weights personally.

Removing sheets one by one.

Scale balanced.

Precision obsessive.

And strangely—

Torlan trusted him more seeing it.

Because guilt may confess.

But craftsmanship tells truth.

At last Quill slid one blank ledger across.

Satisfied.

"These may fool the pedestals."

May.

Marcus did not enjoy may.

No one did.

As team gathered materials, Torlan stood at board.

Under BUILD THE ILLUSION he wrote:

ENTER THE VAULT

Then beneath:

FOLLOW EVERY STEP

He read it.

Felt gravity.

Tomorrow would not be rehearsal.

Nor psychological theater.

Trespass.

Real trespass.

Somewhere in Exchange Spire hidden behind false archives—

Kessler's real books waited,

silent in darkness.

And now—

for the first time—

strangers knew the way in.

Provided

they stepped nowhere wrong.

## Chapter 20 - Into the Vault

They entered Exchange Spire before dawn.

Because Quill said dawn was safest.

Before traffic.

Before audits.

Before routines thickened.

Before the machine fully woke.

Marcus called it

"the hour when bad decisions dress respectably."

No one argued.

The team for vault entry was kept small.

Torlan.

Lillian.

Marcus.

No one extra.

No one expendable.

Alexa remained in the office command room with Quill.

Watching clocks.

Watching timestamp sync.

Watching everything.

As Quill had insisted.

Because too many inside the vault increased risk.

And risk had become arithmetic.

The blank ledgers were wrapped inside ordinary archival transport cases.

Unremarkable.

Heavy.

Exactly right.

As they moved through the lower records annex no one spoke.

Only footsteps.

Muted lights.

Rows of dormant archives.

The place felt less like offices—

more like memory arranged in shelves.

Marcus whispered once:

"This is where bureaucracy goes to die."

Torlan did not answer.

Because now every sound seemed too loud.

At the concealed wall Quill's instructions returned almost physically.

Third shelf support.

Rear latch.

Manual release.

Torlan reached.

Pressed.

Metal shifted.

Softly.

A seam opened.

Invisible door.

Marcus breathed,

"I dislike it even more now."

They entered.

Door shut.

And waited.

No one moved.

Seven seconds.

Exactly.

Torlan counted silently.

One.

Two.

Three—

Heartbeats felt loud.

Seven.

Move.

Three tiles in.

Pause.

Third tile.

Skip black seam.

Marcus stepped over it like crossing a confession.

No one joked.

No one breathed much.

The chamber beyond appeared.

Small.

Cold.

Silent.

Three pedestal shelves.

Just as Quill said.

Two visible ledgers.

Ancient looking.

Heavy.

And beyond—

false rear panel.

The Third Ledger.

Lillian whispered,

"He was right."

Yes.

Torlan approached first pedestal.

Hands steady.

Had to be.

He lifted first ledger onto portable scale.

Weight confirmed.

Matched to blank.

Page removal already exact.

They exchanged ledgers.

Very slowly.

Set replacement down.

No alarm.

Nothing.

Silence.

Second ledger.

Same.

Again.

No alarm.

Marcus muttered,

“We are stealing gravity.”

Even here.

Still Marcus.

Then the false back panel.

Torlan found hidden notch.

Opened.

There.

Third Ledger.

Smaller.

Darker cover.

Almost ordinary.

Most dangerous things often are.

He placed it on scale.

Matched third blank.

Pages adjusted.

Replacement seated.

Panel closed.

Everything as found.

Or so it must seem.

Lillian checked pedestals twice.

Then once more.

Now exit.

Harder part.

Always harder.

Torlan checked chronometer.

Two minutes thirty-eight.

Move.

Return path.

Skip seam.

Entry chamber.

Manual reseal sequence.

Three turns.

Pause.

Reverse latch.

Exactly as taught.

Marcus whispered,

"If door objects…"

No one answered.

Latch settled.

Seal engaged.

Still nothing.

Then—

Torlan's comm bead clicked.

Alexa.

Tight voice.

Timestamp live.

Erase window open.

Four minutes.

Running.

Everything narrowed.

Now.

Move.

They exited concealed wall into archives.

Door hidden again.

As though never there.

Torlan moved to maintenance terminal hidden in adjacent records desk.

Quill's override sequence.

Entered exactly.

No improvisation.

Erase timestamp.

Processing…

A terrible word.

Marcus watched corridor.

Lillian watched clock.

Three minutes twelve.

Three twenty.

Then—

confirmation.

Entry log cleared.

The three of them exhaled almost together.

A human sound.

Earned.

Then footsteps.

Freeze.

Someone in corridor.

A records clerk.

Too early.

Unexpected.

The clerk looked up.

Saw archival transport cases.

Marcus—bless him—spoke first.

Without pause.

"Humidity calibration audit."

The clerk frowned.

Bored.

Nodded.

Left.

Gone.

Only then breathing returned.

Marcus whispered,

"I deserve medals."

They walked out.

Not hurried.

Never hurried.

Because haste confesses.

Routine protects.

That too Quill taught.

At office command room Alexa met them at service entrance.

Did not ask.

Looked at cases.

Then:

"Well."

Torlan nearly laughed.

That word had carried a lot this book.

He set cases down.

Opened one.

The three original ledgers lay there.

Real.

Heavy.

Damning.

For a moment no one spoke.

Because impossible had become possession.

Marcus touched one cover.

Softly.

"We did it."

Torlan looked toward Quill.

Who stood silent.

Almost pale.

Watching his old loyalties become evidence.

Quill finally said,

"Kessler still thinks they're there."

Yes.

For now.

Then Quill added quietly,

"When he learns otherwise…"

He didn't finish.

No need.

Everyone understood.

The clock had started.

Endgame moving.

Later in conference room the ledgers opened.

Pages dense with manual entries.

Payoffs.

Names.

Shell transfers.

Weekly bribes.

Proof.

Not rumors.

Proof.

Doss now had something worth carrying.

Marcus turned pages slowly.

Then looked up.

"We have just stolen the heart from the machine."

Torlan considered.

Then:

"No.

We copied it."

As dawn fully rose through atrium glass, Exchange Spire awakened into ordinary morning.

Employees arrived.

Systems moved.

Kessler perhaps already at his desk.

Confident.

Untouched.

Believing hidden books still sleep beneath false archives.

For now.

Torlan stood over the ledgers.

Thought of Garron.

Thought of Doss.

Thought of Quill's broken loyalty.

And wrote on board beneath ENTER THE VAULT:
THE HEART IS IN HAND
Then below it:
NOW MARK KESSLER
And everyone in the room knew—
the sting had entered its final shape.

## Chapter 21 - The Ownership Challenge

With the ledgers secured, the sting changed character.

Before, they had been stealing truth.

Now—

they had to weaponize it.

Entirely different discipline.

Much harder.

Marcus said this meant they had moved

"from burglary into choreography."

No one disputed him.

The conference room again became war room.

Ledgers open.

Pages marked.

Ownership chains traced.

Names connected.

And in the center of new planning—

Quill.

No longer prisoner.

Not quite ally.

Something harder to define.

Useful.

Complicated.

Human.

He sat at the same conference table where his false interrogation had been staged days before.

A fact Marcus found poetically alarming.

Torlan pointed to one recurring cluster of entries.

"These shell transfers."

Quill nodded.

"Kessler watches those personally."

"And if challenged?"

Quill hesitated.

Then:

"He authenticates."

Everyone felt it.

Alexa leaned forward.

"When would he do that himself?"

Quill looked up.

"When Quill is missing."

He said his own name almost strangely.

As though now studying himself externally.

Marcus muttered,

"That is both useful and unsettling."

Quill explained.

If certain ownership claims were suddenly disputed—

large enough to threaten exposure—

Kessler would have to intervene personally.

Because normally Quill handled such crises.

But Quill, absent—

Kessler would trust no one else.

Torlan said quietly,

"So absence becomes pressure."

Quill nodded.

"Yes."

And perhaps for first time—

he looked almost proud to be helping undo the machine.

The challenge was crafted carefully.

Not too large.

That would smell like attack.

Not too small.

That Kessler delegates.

Precise pressure.

As always.

Lillian built the false ownership contest through shell entities already appearing in ledgers.

Genuine enough to survive scrutiny.

Artificial enough to trigger alarm.

Marcus reviewed it.

"This is fraud against fraud."

Alexa:

"Temporarily."

Of course.

The filing launched at 10:14.

Routine channel.

Routine formatting.

Routine enough.

Then—

waiting.

Always waiting.

No one in conference room pretended calm.

Not even Torlan.

Though he came closest.

Quill watched clock.

Anxious.

For the first time perhaps fearing Kessler's reactions from outside rather than inside.

A different fear.

Then the first sign.

A secure internal bulletin spike.

Ownership escalation.

Moved to executive review.

Fast.

Very fast.

Quill looked up.

"He took it."

Simple words.

Marcus whispered,

"Well."

Useful word again.

Torlan said,

"Now we pull second thread."

Because first challenge alone not enough.

Second pressure.

An audit anomaly triggered through another disputed transfer.

Again routed upward.

Again impossible to ignore.

The machine now being made to tug at itself.

Then Quill stiffened.

"What?"

Alexa asked.

He pointed to incoming executive movement logs.

Kessler had left his office.

Heading to private authentication suite.

Personally.

The mark had moved.

No one breathed for several seconds.

Torlan almost felt the room tilt.

This was it.

The first moment Kessler stepped where they needed.

Marcus said softly,

"He's in."

Yet risk remained.

Because if Kessler sensed trap—

everything dies.

Silence in room became surgical.

Then another development.

Unexpected.

Dangerous.

A message flashed.

Executive inquiry:

Where is Quill?

Everyone froze.

Of course.

Sooner than expected.

Quill went pale.

Torlan read it twice.

Kessler was already noticing absence.

Marcus said,

"He's disturbed."

Quill whispered,

"He never shows disturbance."

The pressure was biting.

Then came the authentication request.

Direct.

Kessler override signature invoked.

Exactly as predicted.

Quill shut his eyes briefly.

"He trusts no one."

Torlan looked at him.

"No."

Quill answered quietly,

"Not even me.

That was my mistake."

The system log confirmed it.

Kessler had authenticated personally.

The sting now possessed him.

Whether he knew it or not.

A strange hush filled room.

Part awe.

Part terror.

Because impossible had happened.

Marcus broke it.

"Someone should note…"

he, pause,

"…we have manipulated a man through accounting paperwork."

Alexa:

History may not honor us correctly."

Needed laughter.

Thin.

Necessary.

But one final move remained.

The Quill sighting.

Your wonderful decoy.

A disguised figure dressed as Quill exiting records levels.

Seen.

Reported.

Then gone.

Designed to provoke exactly what Quill predicted.

Kessler sent pursuit.

Immediately.

Desperately.

Not procedure.

Emotion.

Torlan noticed.

"He's reacting."

Not calculating.

Reacting.

That mattered enormously.

The machine was slipping into man.

Exactly where stings work.

Quill looked shaken.

"He's afraid."

Marcus turned.

"You sound surprised."

Quill answered almost to himself:

"I've never seen him afraid."

Then all at once—

silence.

Because there was nothing more to do.

Only let cascade unfold.

Outside the atrium windows morning had become full day.

Profitthorn moving as always.

Yet somewhere above,

in polished executive rooms,

Kessler now fought invisible pressure from a missing confidant,
contested ownership claims,
phantom sightings,
and his own first taste of uncertainty.
The sting had touched him.
Torlan walked to board.
Under NOW MARK KESSLER he wrote:
THE MARK MOVES
Then beneath:
PRESSURE HOLDS
He stepped back.
Read it.
The machine had begun turning against itself.
And for the first time—
Kessler was no longer only architect.
He was becoming prey.

## Chapter 22 - The Mark Bites Back

For several hours the sting seemed almost too successful.

Torlan distrusted that immediately.

Operations that go too smoothly usually conceal unpaid costs.

Marcus phrased it differently.

"When fate cooperates,

check your wallet."

Both meant the same thing.

The ownership challenge continued rippling through Kessler's systems exactly as Quill predicted.

Authentication requests multiplied.

Emergency routing reviews triggered.

Escalations moved upward.

And increasingly—

Kessler handled them himself.

Every personal intervention tightened the snare.

But it also made him dangerous.

Because intelligent prey notices patterns.

Sooner or later.

And Kessler was very intelligent.

That reminder arrived before noon.

Quill was studying live executive logs when he went still.

Torlan saw it at once.

"What?"

Quill looked up.

"He stopped responding."

"Meaning?"

"Kessler."

Silence.

No one liked that.

At all.

Because frantic men can be predicted.

Calm men thinking—

much harder.

Marcus whispered,

"I preferred him panicking."

Then a new executive action appeared.

Unexpected.

Kessler initiated internal reconciliation review.

Personally.

Quill swore softly.

Everyone looked at him.

Rare event.

Bad sign.

"He's checking underlying structures."

He suspects disturbance.

The room tightened.

For the first time the sting might be seen.

Lillian moved instantly.

"What would he examine first?"

Quill answered without hesitation.

Authorization chains.

Variance flags.

Secondary ledgers.

He looked suddenly pale.

"If he reaches—"

He stopped.

No need finishing.

The stolen books.

The blank replacements.

Everyone understood.

Marcus said quietly,

"Well."

Not humorous now.

Only gravity.

Torlan moved fast.

"If Kessler inspects vault now?"

Quill thought.

Then—

"He won't."

Heads turned.

"Why?"

Because first he'll test whether Quill has betrayed him."

Because Kessler thinks relationally through suspicion.

Not evidence first.

Trust first.

And immediately—

that proved true.

An internal query surfaced.

Priority trace on Quill access credentials.

Kessler was checking Quill.

Not vault.

One breath returned.

Small.

Earned.

Torlan almost smiled.

"He still thinks this is Quill."

Quill answered bitterly,

"He always thinks in betrayal."

Then came the decoy's payoff.

Security reported sighting of Quill-like figure near lower archive sectors.

The false lead.

Seen.

Reported.

Pursued.

And Kessler took it.

Completely.

He diverted security resources.

Personally.

Emotion again overruling structure.

Marcus leaned back.

"He bit."

But Kessler was not finished.

Nor fool.

Minutes later a private executive transmission appeared.

Encrypted.

Unknown recipient.

Quill looked troubled.

"That's unusual."

"How unusual?"

I've only seen him do that…"

He paused,

"…when burning contingencies."

Now that was ominous.

Torlan said nothing.

But remembered.

Burning contingencies.

By midafternoon the ownership challenge escalated into formal authentication confrontation.

Exactly what Quill had hoped.

Exactly what Kessler could not delegate.

His signature appeared repeatedly across disputed chains.

One after another.

Personal involvement deepening.

Each signature—

another self-woven thread.

Lillian quietly said,

"He's authenticating his own cage."

No one improved on that.

Couldn't.

Then—

danger again.

A second pause in Kessler's activity.

Longer this time.

Too long.

Quill stared at logs.

"He's thinking."

Marcus muttered,

"That should be illegal."

Then came the move.

Kessler initiated sealed review in private executive records.

Marcus frowned.

"What is that?"

Quill answered softly.

"He may be preparing failsafes."

Again.

Torlan looked toward closed ledger cases in corner.

The heart in hand.

And suddenly understood.

The sting now raced Kessler's contingencies.

Not just his ignorance.

They needed final pressure.

Now.

Torlan made decision.

"Trigger secondary ownership collapse."

Alexa looked up sharply.

"The bigger one?"

"Yes."

Maybe reckless.

Marcus grinned faintly.

At last.

There was the Torlan I recognize."

The second challenge launched.

Bolder.

Sharper.

And it worked.

Too well.

Kessler abandoned sealed review.

Returned to live authentication crisis.

Hook reset.

Near-win denied.

Quill exhaled visibly.

“He almost saw.”

Torlan nodded.

At dusk the room had that strange exhausted electricity after surviving something unseen.

Marcus sat heavily.

“I would like future missions involving vegetables.”

No one objected.

Then Quill said something quiet.

Unexpected.

“He’s angry now.”

"How do you know?”

Quill looked at Kessler movement logs.

“He’s stopped behaving efficiently.”

That was chilling.

Because Quill would know.

And it meant fear was touching Kessler deeper.

Torlan walked to board.

Under THE MARK MOVES he wrote:

THE MARK STRUGGLES

Then beneath:

FORCE FINAL EXPOSURE

He read it.

Somewhere above,

Kessler sat in polished office light,

thinking perhaps he was regaining control—

while unknowingly signing himself deeper into evidence.

And perhaps,

behind a framed photograph on his wall,

rested a button no one in this room yet knew mattered.

Waiting.

Quietly.

Like all contingencies.

For now.

## Chapter 23 - Delivering the Truth

The ledgers were heavier in Doss's hands than in anyone else's.

Perhaps because he knew what they meant.

Or what they could cost.

He arrived after dark.

Quietly.

No insignia convoy.

No dramatic law enforcement entrance.

Arlen Doss did not arrive like rescue.

He arrived like consequence.

Marcus approved immediately.

The conference room—once fake interrogation chamber, then war room—now held the real evidence stacked in orderly rows.

Manual ledgers.

Cross-referenced pages.

Ownership challenge records.

Authentication logs bearing Kessler's personal signatures.

And Quill's sworn statement.

Real statement this time.

Signed with shaking honesty.

No theater now.

Only truth.

Doss stood over the materials a long while without speaking.

Turning pages.

Reading names.

Following transfers.

Seeing old suspicions become architecture.

At length he closed one ledger.

Looked up.

And said only:

"At last."

No one improved on that.

Couldn't.

He turned another page.

Then another.

Finally:

"This survives burial."

Highest praise possible.

Torlan felt the room ease.

Just slightly.

Earned.

Doss looked toward Quill.

Long pause.

"You built part of this."

Not accusation.

Fact.

Quill nodded.

"Yes."

Doss studied him.

Then:

"And now you are undoing it."

Quill looked down.

Almost unable to bear mercy.

Doss gathered documents into sealed evidence cases.

No flourish.

Only precision.

Then said:

"Once I move…"

He looked around room.

"…there is no partial version of this."

Meaning:

when arrests begin,

they begin.

All at once.

Exactly as required.

Quill had insisted on simultaneity.

If warned,

too many disappear.

Doss agreed.

Torlan asked,

"How far can you carry it?"

Doss answered with that granite calm:

"As far as law survives."

Then he added:

"And farther if necessary."

Marcus whispered,

"I may adopt him."

No one disagreed.

The arrest architecture formed quickly.

Quietly.

Warrants prepared.

Multi-site seizures.

Coordinated detentions.

Financial locks.

Communication freezes.

Every thread designed to move at once.

The machine to be struck everywhere.

Not one point.

Doss finally looked at Torlan.

"When do we move?"

Torlan answered:

"When Kessler authenticates one last time."

The final trap.

Yes.

Because the sting still needed last tightening.

Kessler must step once farther.

Personally.

Into evidence.

And so they waited.

Again.

Always waiting.

Near dawn the final ownership escalation launched.

Quill's idea.

A dispute only Kessler would touch himself.

And he did.

Exactly.

His personal override entered system.

Captured.

Time stamped.

Recorded.

Doss watched the confirmation appear.

Then closed the evidence case.

"Move."

One word.

History changed.

Operations unfolded instantly.

Not loudly.

Like dominoes.

Silent.

Precise.

Reports began arriving through secure channels.

Regional detentions confirmed.

Shell administrators secured.

Archive seizures underway.

Transfer hubs frozen.

Marcus stared.

"We appear to be toppling a government."

"Only part of one," Alexa said.

Then—

the message.

Executive security en route Kessler suite.

Everyone stilled.

This was it.

No one breathed much.

Seconds dragged.

Then another message.

Suite entered.

Subject contained.

Marcus exhaled.

"Well."

This time almost prayer.

But—

not yet.

Then came the moment.

Kessler, seeing officers entering, rose.

Moved to wall.

Lifted framed photograph.

Behind it—

hidden switch.

Quill went white.

"The vault failsafe."

Kessler pressed it.

Somewhere far below a signal turned.

On monitoring feed—

small green indicator above vault status turned red.

Destruction initiated.

Kessler's near-win.

He thinks he saved himself.

For three terrible seconds even this room froze.

Then another law officer in Kessler's suite lifted a folder.

Transmission audio cracked through.

Calm voice:

"No cause for concern.

We can make copies from the originals.

The ones in our possession since yesterday."

Silence.

Then Marcus whispered,

"Oh…"

Perfect.

On monitor—

Kessler's expression changed.

Confidence draining.

The grin gone.

Destroyed not by force—

by irrelevance.

His contingency had fired too late.

Doss almost smiled.

Almost.

Then came mass arrest confirmations.

One after another.

Wave becoming flood.

The machine collapsing inward.

Quill sat down hard.

As though years left him at once.

Torlan looked at him.

"You all right?"

Quill answered faintly,

"I think…"

he paused,

"…I just watched an empire end."

By noon Garron Vale's emergency review was reopened.

Doss arranged it personally.

As arrests continued, Doss gathered his cases.

Prepared to leave.

At door he stopped.

Turned.

Looked at Torlan.

"You built a sting."

Doss paused.

Then:

"Now let law finish it."

Then looked toward Quill.

Long silence.

No hostility.

No softness either.

Justice.

Balanced.

At length Doss said,

"Mr. Quill."

Quill stood.

He had known this moment was coming.

Of course.

He extended his hands before being asked.

A small gesture.

But telling.

One officer stepped forward.

Steel cuffs clicked closed.

The sound was quiet.

Yet somehow immense.

Marcus looked down.

Alexa did not.

Torlan watched Quill carefully.

No resistance.

No protest.

Only a strange weariness.

And perhaps—

relief.

Doss said quietly,

"You will answer for what you helped build."

Quill nodded.

"Yes."

Then after a pause:

"But Kessler answers too."

Doss:

"He will."

Before being led out Quill turned once toward Torlan.

Unexpected.

Almost awkward.

As though unfamiliar with gratitude.

"I believed intelligence excused corruption."

He gave faint bitter smile.

"You corrected that."

Torlan answered:

"You corrected it."

Quill nodded once.

Enough.

Then Doss led him toward door.

In cuffs.

Not as rescued informant.

Not innocent accountant.

As guilty man cooperating with truth.

At threshold Quill paused once.

Looked back at the false holding room.

The interrogation chamber.

The absurd stage that undid an empire.

And almost incredulously said,

"All this…"

small shake of head,

"…began with coffee."

Marcus:

"Most dangerous things do."

Then Quill was gone.

Escorted into law.

Where he belonged.

And somehow the room felt emptier than anyone expected.

Because he had become part of the moral weight.

## Chapter 24 - Garron Goes Home

The release order came without ceremony.

Which somehow suited Garron Vale.

Too much had been stolen from his life for justice now to need trumpet blasts.

It arrived as paper.

Signature.

Seal.

Door unlocking.

Simple things.

Yet miraculous.

Doss sent the message personally.

Three words.

**He walks today.**

Marcus read it aloud in the conference room.

No one spoke for several seconds.

Then he said softly:

"Well."

This time the word felt almost sacred.

Torlan looked out through the atrium glass.

For the first time in many weeks—

nothing pressed.

No clock.

No trap.

No mark.

Only aftermath.

And home.

They met Garron outside the detention complex just before dusk.

He stepped through the gate carrying one small case.

Twenty years had once stretched before him.

Now only open sky.

He paused just beyond the threshold.

As if unsure whether freedom should be trusted.

Torlan crossed first.

No speeches.

Just offered a hand.

Garron looked at it.

Then took it.

Grip hard.

Wordless.

Enough.

Marcus muttered quietly,

"I had prepared something heroic."

Alexa:

"No you hadn't."

Then Garron laughed.

First real laugh any of them had heard from him.

And somehow the whole long operation felt worth it for that alone.

They drove him home at sunset.

None of them spoke much.

They didn't need to.

Some moments resist commentary.

This was one.

As the transport turned into the residential lane Garron went still.

House lights glowed.

Porch lit.

Waiting.

And there—

his family.

Wife.

Children.

Waiting exactly as he once said they would.

They never doubted him.

Garron whispered,

"They stayed."

Almost disbelief.

Torlan answered quietly,

"They said they would."

Then Garron stepped out.

His wife crossed the yard before he fully cleared the transport.

No restraint.

No staged dignity.

Just years collapsing.

She threw arms around him.

Held on as if refusing time permission ever again.

His children close behind.

No one in Torlan's team looked directly at one another.

A wise decision.

Marcus inspected the sky with suspicious intensity.

Alexa seemed fascinated by gravel.

After a while Garron turned back toward them.

Unable to speak at first.

Then only:

"You brought me home."

Torlan shook his head.

"Truth did."

His youngest—no longer youngest really—stepped forward.

"We told everyone Father would come back."

That nearly undid Marcus.

Though he would deny it.

Inside, Garron insisted they stay.

There was food.

Simple table.

Crowded.

Warm.

Nothing grand.

Which made it grand.

Children asking questions.

Stories beginning.

Ordinary life doing extraordinary healing.

Torlan watched and thought—

this is why machines must fall.

For tables like this.

Later, on the porch as evening deepened, Garron stood beside Torlan.

Quiet.

Then said:

"I spent years believing truth had lost."

Carron paused.

"I was wrong."

Torlan looked out over darkening lane.

"It sometimes walks slowly."

Garron smiled.

Inside laughter drifted through open door.

Before leaving Garron handed Torlan a folded paper.

"What is it?"

"The letter my son brought me in prison."

The one about waiting.

Torlan looked surprised.

"Why give me this?"

Garron answered:

"So you remember what your sting was for."

On return to the office—now half dismantled, false cell gone, maps coming down—the team stood in strange quiet.

Marcus looked around.

"I feel almost disappointed no one is being abducted."

Alexa:

"Concerning."

Lillian:

"Persistent pattern."

Torlan erased the board slowly.

Trap him.

Make Kessler the mark.

Build the illusion.

The machine falls.

One by one.

Then at center wrote only:

HOME

And beneath it:

WORTH IT

No one suggested improvement.

There wasn't one.

As the others drifted out, Doss arrived once more.

Unexpected.

Carrying a slim sealed file.

He set it on table.

Torlan looked at it.

"What is that?"

Doss's expression turned harder.

"The top name."

Torlan opened folder.

One page.

One name.

And beneath it—

a symbol he had seen once before.

From Halvern.

Old shadows returning.

He looked up.

Doss said only:

"Kessler was not the ceiling."

Silence.

Marcus sighed.

"I knew peace was suspicious."

Doss moved toward door.

Then paused.

"You'll want to rest first."

"Before deciding whether to go looking."

Then he left.

Torlan stood with the file in hand.

The next mystery whispering.

But not yet.

Not tonight.

Tonight belonged elsewhere.

He folded file closed.

Turned off lights.

And walked out.

Outside Profitthorn glimmered under evening stars.

The machine quieter.

The wounds not all healed.

But something restored.

And sometimes, Torlan thought,

victory is not bringing down what is corrupt.

It is bringing someone home.

The sting had done both.

For now, that was enough.

## Chapter 25 - The Second Door Opens

The report did not arrive loudly.

Important things rarely did.

It entered through secure channels in the quiet hour after midnight, routed with the kind of authority that bypassed ordinary systems without leaving visible disturbance.

Torlan almost missed it.

Almost.

He sat alone in the half-dismantled office, the war room now nearly returned to ordinary rooms.

Maps gone.

False cell removed.

The interrogation lamp boxed away.

Only one board remained.

Mostly erased.

One word still visible:

HOME.

He had meant to leave.

Instead—

the secure terminal chimed.

Once.

Softly.

He opened the message.

Classification seals.

Doss.

Attached file.

Minimal note.

**Thought you should see this before I bury it.**

Torlan opened the file.

Read once.

Then again.

Slower.

The room seemed quieter after.

The name meant little at first glance.

No public figure.

No celebrated magnate.

No obvious ruler.

Which somehow made it worse.

Power often hides that way.

Below the name—

a symbol.

Simple.

Geometric.

Ancient looking.

And Torlan froze.

Because he had seen it before.

Halvern.

Long ago.

Fragmented records.

Dismissed traces.

The same symbol.

The same mark.

Not coincidence.

Impossible.

The door opened behind him.

Marcus entered carrying coffee.

Stopped immediately.

"That is not your ordinary face."

Torlan slid the file across.

Marcus read.

Silence.

Then:

"No."

Softly.

As if refusing mathematics.

Alexa arrived moments later.

Read.

Looked up.

"Kessler wasn't the top."

Torlan answered quietly,

"No."

Marcus sank into chair.

For once without commentary.

At length he said,

"I had just begun trusting peace."

Torlan reopened the file.

There was more.

Not much.

Just enough.

Financial traces extending beyond Profitthorn.

Shell structures predating Kessler.

References to something called **The Directorate Node.**

And one line from Doss:

**Kessler may have been management.**

**Not authorship.**

That line chilled the room.

Because it redefined everything.

Alexa whispered,

"We touched an edge again."

Torlan looked toward darkened window.

Lights of Profitthorn glittered beyond.

Same city.

Changed city.

And perhaps a less understood city.

Marcus finally recovered enough to mutter,

"I dislike second doors."

No one improved on it.

Couldn't.

Torlan turned final page.

One notation near bottom.

Single phrase:

**Profitthorn was never the center.**

Silence.

Long.

Then Marcus:

"Well."

The word had survived every catastrophe.

Still useful.

Alexa folded arms.

"What now?"

Torlan considered.

A long time.

Then closed the file.

"Not tonight."

It was important to let this night remain what it was—a night for victories earned.

He set the file aside.

It belonged to Garron home again,

to Kessler fallen,

to truth surviving.

Not yet to next shadows.

Marcus looked relieved.

Profoundly.

"Excellent. I was tired."

They laughed.

Quietly.

Like people who had earned the right.

Later, after they left, Torlan remained alone.

He stepped to the old board.

Looked at the word:

HOME.

Then beneath it—

he wrote one final line.

SECOND DOOR

And beneath that:

NOT YET CLOSED

He stood back.

Read it.

A long time.

Outside the city shimmered.

Ships crossing distant lanes.

Lights moving like thoughts.

Somewhere in secure detention Kessler sat learning he had not even been as powerful as he imagined.

Somewhere Doss was burying files too dangerous for open shelves.

And somewhere—

far beyond this quiet room—

a larger machine may still be turning.

Patiently waiting.

Torlan switched off the lights.

Picked up the file.

And walked toward the door.

At threshold he paused.

Looked once more at the dark room where a sting had begun over coffee and ended with empires bent.

Then he smiled faintly.

Because perhaps Marcus was right.

Danger did seem fond of doors.

He closed the office behind him.

And somewhere—

very far away—

another one opened.

## Case Summary — The Hearthridge Operation

What began as a question about one powerful man became the exposure of an entire hidden structure.

Torlan Tarsen and his team came to Profitthorn believing Adrian Kessler might be a dangerous executive operating behind layers of respectable commerce. What they uncovered was something far darker—a machine built on fraud, coercion, buried records, and lives quietly destroyed.

Their first discoveries led them to Garron Vale, a former insider falsely imprisoned after trying to expose corruption years earlier. Through Garron's testimony, an honest officer named Arlen Doss was found—one trustworthy place where truth could be delivered when the time came.

The turning point came with Marven Quill.

Once Kessler's cold and calculating confidant, Quill was drawn into a carefully staged deception that convinced him Kessler had sacrificed him. What began as a psychological sting became a confession, then cooperation. Through Quill, the team discovered the hidden vault and recovered the real ledgers—the evidence at the heart of Kessler's empire.

From there the operation shifted.

Using disputed ownership claims, authentication traps, decoys, and pressure designed to force Kessler's own hand, the team turned his need for control against him. Each move drew him deeper into self-authenticated evidence until arrests could be launched across the network at once.

Kessler fell.

His failsafes failed.

His machine collapsed inward.

Garron Vale was freed.

Quill entered custody to answer for his own part in what had been built.

And Arlen Doss carried the evidence into the hands of law.

But the operation uncovered one final truth:

Kessler was not the ceiling.

Only a layer.

Only a manager.

A second door stands open.

And beyond it—

someone else may still be waiting.

---

**Operational Outcomes**
**Primary Target:** Adrian Kessler — Contained

**Fraud Network:** Disrupted

**Evidence Recovered:** Three original ledgers secured

**Wrongful Conviction:** Garron Vale exonerated

**Cooperating Defendant:** Marven Quill in custody

**Lead Investigator:** Arlen Doss continuing inquiry

**Unresolved Threat:** "Directorate Node" active status unknown

**Operation Status:** Successful

**Investigation Status:** Ongoing

## The Final Sting

The Hearthridge Operation is over.

Kessler has fallen.

But some victories do not end a war.

They reveal its true scale.

A buried file.

An older symbol.

A name above the architect.

And a whispered warning:

**Profitthorn was never the center.**

Some machines are built to hide.

Others are built to survive exposure.

Torlan Tarsen has just discovered there may be a system older, larger, and far more patient than anything he has yet faced.

And somewhere beyond the first sting—

another game is already in motion.

Another trap.

Another architect.

Another door.

**The investigation continues…**

---

**Coming Next in the Torlan Tarsen Files**

**Book 7 — The Final Sting**

*(working title)*

Sometimes the most dangerous secret

is the one behind the secret you just uncovered.

## Principal Characters

**Torlan Tarsen**

Strategist, investigator, and architect of the sting against Kessler. Analytical, patient, and willing to let truth move slowly when necessary.

**Alexa Voss**

Systems analyst and operational planner. Precise, perceptive, and often the quiet center of the team's discipline.

**Marcus Vale**

Field operative, skeptic, and improviser whose humor often surfaces when pressure is highest. Frequently sees danger first by joking about it.

**Lillian Mercer**

Research specialist and logistical architect behind the ownership challenge and vault operation. Detail-driven and exceptionally calm under pressure.

**Arlen Doss**

An honest officer who becomes the trusted legal channel for the evidence uncovered in the Hearthridge Operation.

**Garron Vale**

Former executive whistleblower wrongfully imprisoned after challenging corruption. His testimony becomes a turning point in the investigation.

**Marven Quill**
Former confidant and hidden architect within Kessler's network. Both guilty participant and crucial witness in the collapse of the machine he helped build.

**Adrian Kessler**
Powerful executive strategist whose hidden fraud system reaches far beyond ordinary corporate crime. The principal target of the sting.

---

**Emerging Threats**

**The Directorate Node**
A shadow structure referenced only in fragments—suggesting Kessler may have served something larger.

**The Unnamed Top Figure**
A name discovered only after Kessler's fall… and the reason a second investigation may be unavoidable.

## About the Series

**The Torlan Tarsen Files**
Some battles are fought with force.
Others are won with truth.

**The Torlan Tarsen Files** is a science-fiction suspense series built around hidden systems, strategic investigations, and carefully constructed stings against powerful forces operating in shadow. At the center is **Torlan Tarsen**—an analytical investigator whose greatest weapon is often patience—joined by a small team of allies who understand that bringing down corruption sometimes requires more than courage. It requires precision.

Set among trade hubs, corporate strongholds, hidden archives, and layered conspiracies, these novels blend mystery, intelligence-driven suspense, moral stakes, and the slow-burn tension of operations where one wrong move can collapse everything.

Each story stands on its own, while also advancing a larger unfolding mystery.

Themes of loyalty, justice, sacrifice, deception, and truth run through the series—along with moments of humor, friendship, and hope amid dangerous work.

If you enjoy intelligent thrillers, conspiracies unraveled step by step, and stories where strategy matters as much as action, **The Torlan Tarsen Files** invites you deeper.

## Reading Order

**The Torlan Tarsen Files**

A character-driven science fiction suspense series where intelligence, patience, and moral courage often matter more than force.
Each novel stands on its own while contributing to a larger journey.

**Book 1 — Torlan Tarsen: Raised Among Giants**

On the high-gravity world of Cyrion, a lost child is shaped into the man who will one day face impossible problems with unusual wisdom.

**Book 2 — Torlan Tarsen: The Havenfall Accord**

A fragile colony, two rival civilizations, and one chance to turn a battlefield into peace.

**Book 3 — Torlan Tarsen: The Lost Expedition — Asterra-9**

A rescue mission becomes a mystery of shifting structures, hidden patterns, and discoveries that challenge explanation.

**Book 4 — Torlan Tarsen: The Canyon Ascent**

A crash in a deadly canyon tests survival, leadership, and the cost of clear decisions under pressure.

---

**The Profitthorn Arc**

**Book 5 — Torlan Tarsen: The First Sting**

A carefully designed operation turns a hidden machine of corruption against itself.

**Book 6 — Torlan Tarsen: The Perfect Sting**

Kessler controls the machine. Torlan and his team must construct a perfect operation—one so precise it can succeed only if Kessler himself chooses the wrong move.

**Coming Next**

**Book 7 — Torlan Tarsen: The Final Sting**

## About the Author

**Russell McFall** writes clean, character-driven science fiction adventures where intelligence, courage, and moral conviction matter as much as action.

After a long career in software development, Russell turned more fully to the stories he had been telling for years—stories shaped by a love of mystery, problem-solving, and the belief that even in dangerous worlds, truth and character still matter.

His fiction ranges from the adventurous **Space Cadet Legacy** books to the more strategic suspense of **The Torlan Tarsen Files**, where layered conspiracies, careful stings, and quiet acts of courage often carry greater power than force.

Many of his stories first began as bedtime adventures told to his children during years of homeschooling, and that spirit of wonder, humor, and thoughtful heroism still shapes his writing today.

Russell also writes biblical reflections and nonfiction works centered on truth, faith, and understanding Scripture.

He and his wife Debbie have been married many years and remain grateful for the Lord's faithfulness through every season.

When not writing, Russell enjoys developing new story worlds, studying Scripture, and asking what hidden problem a patient mind might solve next.

## Also by Russell McFall

*Ordained Path Books*

Clean Science Fiction and Inspirational Writing for Thoughtful Readers

---

### A Torlan Tarsen Adventure

- *Character-driven science fiction of leadership, problem-solving, and quiet strength*
- **Torlan Tarsen — Raised Among Giants**
- **Torlan Tarsen — The Havenfall Accord**
- **Torlan Tarsen — The Lost Expedition — Asterra-9**
- **Torlan Tarsen — The Canyon Ascent**
- **Torlan Tarsen — The First Sting**
- **Torlan Tarsen — The Perfect Sting**

---

### Contemporary Fiction and Short Stories

Stories of Community, Memory, and Hope

- **Squirrel Creek Estates — Where the Porch Lights Stay On**
- **The World That Chose**

---

### The Space Cadet Richard Series

*Where the Legacy Began*

- **The Final Countdown**
- **The Dunes of Dinkytown**
- **The Mastermind's Maze**

---

**The Space Cadet Legacy Series**

*Over 30+ novels of courage, friendship, and discovery — including*

- **The First Gate**
- **Welcome Back, Player**
- **Flibber's Journey Home**
- **Stronger Together**
- **Phasegate Rising**
- **The Makers' Handshake**
- **Optimized**

*(New missions continuing.)*

---

**Literary Humor and Reflections**

**Serious Nonsense — Sanity Sold Separately**

---

**Devotional and Reflection Books**

- **Remembering God's Help — Stone by Stone**
- **Attributes of God**
- **This Is My Story, This Is My Song**
- **Lives of Faith**
- **Foundations of Faith**

---

Russell McFall writes clean fiction and thoughtful reflections designed to uplift the heart, sharpen the mind, and remind every reader that light still wins.

www.ingramcontent.com/pod-product-compliance
Lightning Source LLC
LaVergne TN
LVHW010649110826
845149LV00014B/3001

* 9 7 8 1 9 7 2 7 2 4 2 0 0 *